PRAISE FOR THE NOVELS OF CONNIE WILLIS

DOOMSDAY BOOK
Winner of the Nebula and Hugo Awards

"A tour de force ... Ms. Willis displays impressive control of her material."
—*The New York Times Book Review*

"The world of 1348 burns in the mind's eye and every character alive in that year is a fully realized being. ... It becomes possible to feel ... that Connie Willis did, in fact, over the five years *Doomsday Book* took her to write, open a window to another world, and that she saw something there."
—*The Washington Post Book World*

"A stunning novel that encompasses both suffering and hope."
—*The Denver Post*

"Splendid work—brutal, gripping, and genuinely harrowing, the product of diligent research, fine writing, and well-honed instincts, that should appeal far beyond the usual science-fiction constituency."
—*Kirkus Reviews* (starred review)

"A splendid job ... intense and frightening."
—*Detroit Free Press*

"One of the best genre novels of the year ... Cannot be too highly recommended or too widely read."
—*Booklist*

"A leading candidate for science fiction novel of the year ... Profoundly tragic, powerfully moving."
—*Star Tribune*, Minneapolis

"The clarity and consistency of Willis's writing, as well as her deft storytelling ability, place her among this decade's most promising writers. . . . [*Doomsday Book*] rates special attention."   —*Library Journal*

LINCOLN'S DREAMS
*Winner of the John W. Campbell Award
for Best Science Fiction Novel*

"A love story on more than one level, and Ms. Willis does justice to them all. It was only toward the end of the book that I realized how much tension had been generated, how engrossed I was in the characters, how much I cared about their fates."
   —*The New York Times Book Review*

"A tantalizing mix of history and scientific speculation . . . Willis tells this tale with clarity and assurance. . . . Her prose is impeccable."   —*San Francisco Chronicle*

"Fulfills all the expectations of those who have admired her award-winning short fiction."
   —*Los Angeles Times*

"*Lincoln's Dreams* is a novel of classical proportions and virtues . . . humane and moving."
   —*The Washington Post Book World*

"*Lincoln's Dreams* is not so much written as sculpted, a . . . tale of love and war as moving as a distant roll of drums. . . . No one has reproduced the past that haunts the present any better than Connie Willis."
   —*The Christian Science Monitor*

Uncharted Territory

CONNIE WILLIS

BANTAM BOOKS
New York • Toronto • London • Sydney • Auckland

UNCHARTED TERRITORY

A Bantam Spectra Book/July 1994

*SPECTRA and the portrayal of a boxed "s"
are trademarks of Bantam Books,
a division of Bantam Doubleday Dell Publishing Group, Inc.*

*All rights reserved.
Copyright © 1994 by Connie Willis.
Cover art copyright © 1994 by Gary Ruddell.
Map design by GDS/Jeffrey L. Ward.
Book design by Mierre.
No part of this book may be reproduced or transmitted in any
form or by any means, electronic or mechanical, including
photocopying, recording, or by any information storage and
retrieval system, without permission in writing from the publisher.
For information address: Bantam Books.*

ISBN 0-553-56294-0

Published simultaneously in the United States and Canada

*Bantam Books are published by Bantam Books, a division of Bantam
Doubleday Dell Publishing Group, Inc. Its trademark, consisting of the
words "Bantam Books" and the portrayal of a rooster, is Registered in
U.S. Patent and Trademark Office and in other countries. Marca Reg-
istrada. Bantam Books, 1540 Broadway, New York, New York 10036.*

PRINTED IN THE UNITED STATES OF AMERICA

OPM   0 9 8 7 6 5 4 3 2 1

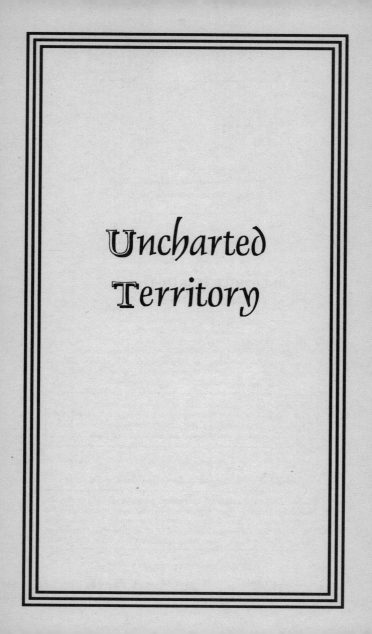

Uncharted Territory

UNCHARTED TERRITORY

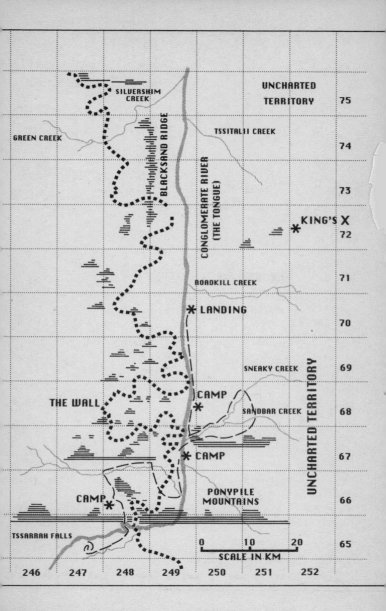

Expedition 183: Day 19

We were still three kloms from King's X when Carson spotted the dust. "What on hell's that?" he said, leaning forward over his pony's pommelbone and pointing at nothing that I could see.

"Where?" I said.

"Over there. All that dust."

I still couldn't see anything except the pinkish ridge that hid King's X, and a couple of luggage grazing on the scourbrush, and I told him so.

"My shit, Fin, what do you mean you can't—" he said, disgusted. "Hand me the binocs."

"You've got 'em," I said. "I gave 'em to you yesterday. Hey, Bult!" I called up to our scout.

He was hunched over the log on his pony's saddlebone, punching in numbers. *"Bult!"* I shouted. "Do you see any dust up ahead?"

He still didn't look up, which didn't surprise me. He was busy doing his favorite thing, tallying up fines.

"I gave the binocs back to you," Carson said. "This morning when we packed up."

"This morning?" I said. "This morning you were in such an all-fired hurry to get back to King's X and meet the new loaner you probably went off and left 'em lying in camp. What's her name again? Evangeline?"

"Evelyn Parker," he said. "I was not in a hurry."

"How come you ran up two-fifty in fines breaking camp, then?"

"Because Bult's on some kind of fining *spree* the last few days," he said. "And the only hurry I've been in is to finish up this expedition before every dime of our wages goes for fines, which looks like a lost cause now that you lost the binocs."

"You weren't in a hurry yesterday," I said. "Yesterday you were all ready to ride fifty kloms north on the off-chance of running into Wulfmeier, and then C.J. calls and tells you the new loaner's in and her name's Eleanor, and all of a sudden you can't get home fast enough."

"*Evelyn*," Carson said, getting red in the face, "and I still say Wulfmeier's surveying that sector. You just don't like loaners."

"You're right about that," I said. "They're more trouble than they're worth." I've never met a loaner yet that was worth taking along, and the females are the worst.

They come in one variety: whiners. They spend every minute of the expedition complaining—about the outdoor plumbing and the dust and Bult and having to ride ponies and everything else they can think of. The last one spent the whole expedition yowling about "terrocentric enslaving imperialists," meaning Carson and me, and how we'd corrupted the "simple, noble indigenous sentients," meaning Bult, which was bad enough, but then she latched onto Bult and told him our presence "defiled the very atmosphere of the planet," and Bult started trying to fine us for breathing.

"I laid the binocs right next to your bedroll, Fin," Carson said, reaching behind him to rummage in his pack.

"Well, I never saw 'em."

"That's because you're half-blind," he said. "You can't even see a cloud of dust when it's coming right at you."

Well, as a matter of fact, we'd been arguing long enough that now I could, a kicked-up line of pinkish cloud close to the ridge.

"What do you think it is? A dust tantrum?" I said, even though a tantrum would've been meandering all over the place, not keeping to a line.

"I don't know," he said, putting his hand up to shade his eyes. "A stampede maybe."

The only fauna around here were luggage, and they didn't stampede in dry weather like this, and anyway the cloud wasn't wide enough for a stampede. It looked like the dust churned up by a rover, or a gate opening.

I kicked my terminal on and asked for whereabouts on the gatecrashers. I'd shown Wulfmeier on Dazil yesterday when Carson'd been so set on going after him, and now the whereabouts showed him on Starting Gate, which meant he probably wasn't either place. But he'd have to be crazy to open a gate this close to a King's X, even if there was anything underneath here—which there wasn't, I'd already run terrains and subsurfaces—especially knowing we were on our way home.

I squinted at the dust, wondering if I should ask for a verify. I could see now it was moving fast, which meant it wasn't a gate, or a pony, and the dust was too low for the heli. "Looks like the rover," I said. "Maybe the new loaner—what was her name? Ernestine?—is as jumped for you as you are for her, and she's coming out here to meet you. You better comb your mustache."

He wasn't paying any attention. He was still rummaging in his pack, looking for the binocs. "I laid 'em right next to your bedroll when you were loading the ponies."

"Well, I didn't see 'em," I said, watching the dust. It was a good thing it wasn't a stampede, it would have run us over while we stood there arguing about the binocs. "Maybe Bult took 'em."

"Why on hell would Bult take 'em?" Carson bellowed. "His are a hell of a lot fancier than ours."

They were, with selective scans and programmed polarizers, and Bult had hung them around the second joint of his neck and was peering through them at the dust. I rode up next to him. "Can you see what's making the dust?" I asked.

He didn't take the binocs down from his eyes. "Disturbance of land surface," he said severely. "Fine of one hundred."

I should've known it. Bult could've cared less about what was making the dust so long as he could get a fine out of it. "You can't fine us for dust unless we make it," I said. "Give me the binocs."

He bent his neck double, took the binocs off, and handed them to me, and then hunched over his log again. "Forcible confiscation of property," he said into his log. "Twenty-five."

"Confiscation!" I said. "You're not going to fine me

with confiscating anything. I *asked* if I could borrow them."

"Inappropriate tone and manner in speaking to an indigenous person," he said into the log. "Fifty."

I gave up and put the binocs up to my eyes. The cloud of dust looked like it was right on top of me, but no clearer. I upped the resolution and took another look. "It's the rover," I called to Carson, who'd gotten off his pony and was taking everything out of his pack.

"Who's driving?" he said. "C.J.?"

I hit the polarizers to screen out the dust and took another look. "What'd you say this loaner's name was, Carson?"

"Evelyn. Did C.J. bring her out with her?"

"It's not C.J. driving," I said.

"Well, who on hell is it? Don't tell me one of the indidges stole the rover again."

"Unfair accusation of indigenous person," Bult said. "Seventy-five."

"You know how you always get mad over the indidges giving things the wrong names?" I said.

"What on hell does that have to do with who's driving the rover?" Carson said.

"Because it looks like the indidges aren't the only ones doing it," I said. "It looks like now Big Brother's doing it, too."

"Give me those binocs," he said, grabbing for 'em.

"Forcible confiscation of property," I said, holding them away from him. "Looks like you could've taken your time this morning and not gone off in such a hurry you forgot ours."

I handed the binocs back to Bult, and just to be contrary, he handed them to Carson, but the rover was close enough now we didn't need them.

It roared up in a cloud of dust, skidded to a halt right on top of a roadkill, and the driver jumped out and strode over to us without even waiting for the dust to clear.

"Carson and Findriddy, I presume," he said, grinning.

Now usually when we meet a loaner, they don't have eyes for anybody but Bult (or C.J., if she's there and the loaner's a male), especially if Bult's unfolding himself off his pony the way he was now, straightening out his back joints one after the other till he looks like a big pink Erector set. Then, while the loaners are still picking their jaws up out of the dirt, one of the ponies keels over or else drops a pile the size of the rover. It's tough to compete with. So we usually get noticed last or else have to say something like, "Bult's only dangerous when he senses your fear," to get their attention.

But this loaner didn't so much as glance at Bult. He came straight over to me and shook hands. "How do you do," he said eagerly, pumping my hand. "I'm Dr. Parker, the new member of your survey team."

"I'm Fin—" I started.

"Oh, I know who *you* are, and I can't *tell* you what an *honor* it is to meet you, Dr. Findriddy!"

He let go of my hand and started in on Carson's. "When C.J. told me you weren't back yet, I couldn't wait till you arrived to meet you," he said, jerking Carson's hand up and down. "Findriddy and Carson! The famous planetary surveyors! I can't believe I'm shaking hands with you, Dr. Carson!"

"It's kind of hard for me to believe, too," Carson said.

"What'd you say your name was, again?" I asked.

"Dr. Parker," he said, grabbing my hand to shake it again. "Dr. Findriddy, I've read all your—"

"Fin," I said, "and this is Carson. There's only four of us on the planet, counting you, so there's not much call for fancy titles. What do you want us to call you?" but he'd already left off pumping my hand and was staring past Carson.

"Is that the Wall?" he said, pointing at a bump on the horizon.

"Nope," I said. "That's Three Moon Mesa. The Wall's twenty kloms the other side of the Tongue."

"Are we going to see it on the expedition?"

"Yeah. We have to cross it to get into uncharted territory," I said.

"Great. I can't wait to see the Wall and the silvershim trees," he said, looking down at Carson's boots, "and the cliff where Carson lost his foot."

"How do you know about all this stuff?" I asked.

He looked back and forth at us in amazement. "Are you kidding? Everybody knows about Carson and Findriddy! You're famous! Dr. Findriddy, you're—"

"*Fin,*" I said. "What do you want us to call you?"

"Evelyn," he said. He looked from one to the other of us. "It's a British name. My mother was from England. Only they pronounce it with a long *e*."

"And you're an exozoologist?" I said.

"Socioexozoologist. My speciality's sex."

"C.J.'s the one you want then," I said. "She's our resident expert."

He blushed a nice pink. "I've already met her."

"She told you her name yet?" I said.

"Her name?" he said blankly.

"What C.J. stands for," I said. "She must be slipping," I said to Carson.

Carson ignored me. "If you're an expert on sex," Carson said, looking over at Bult, who was heading for the rover, "you can help us tell which one Bult is."

"I thought the Boohteri were a simple two-sex species," Evelyn said.

"They are," Carson said, "only we can't tell which one's which."

"All their equipment's on the inside," I said, "not like C.J.'s. It—"

"Speaking of which, did she have supper ready?" Carson said. "Not that it makes any difference to us. At this rate we'll still be out here tomorrow morning."

"Oh. Of course," Evelyn said, looking dismayed, "you're eager to get back to headquarters. I didn't mean to keep you. I was just so excited to actually meet you!" He started off for the rover. Bult was hunched over the front tire. He unfolded three leg joints when Evelyn came up. "Damage to indigenous fauna," he said. "Seventy-five."

Evelyn said to me, "Have I done something wrong?"

"Hard not to in these parts," I said. "Bult, you can't fine Evelyn for running over a roadkill."

"Running over—" Evelyn said. He leapt in the rover and roared it back off the roadkill, and then jumped out again. "I didn't see it!" he said, peering at its flattened brown body. "I didn't mean to kill it! Honestly, I—"

"You can't kill a roadkill just by parking a rover on it," I said, poking it with my toe. "You can't even wake it up."

Bult pointed at the tire tracks Evelyn'd just made. "Disruption of land surface. Twenty-five."

"Bult, you can't fine Evelyn," I said. "He's not a member of the expedition."

"Disruption of land surface," Bult said, pointing at the tire tracks.

"Shouldn't I have come out here in the rover?" Evelyn said worriedly.

"Sure you should," I said, clapping him on the shoulder, " 'cause now you can give me a ride home. Carson, bring in my pony for me." I opened the door of the rover.

"I'm not getting stuck out here with the ponies while you ride back in style," Carson said. "*I'll* ride in with Evelyn, and *you* bring the ponies."

"Can't we all go back in the rover?" Evelyn said, looking upset. "We could tie the ponies to the back."

"The rover can't go that slow," Carson muttered.

"You've got no reason to get back early, Carson," I said. "I've got to check the purchase orders, and the pursuants, *and* fill out the report on the binocs you lost." I got in the rover and sat down.

"*I* lost?" Carson said, getting red in the face again. "I laid 'em—"

"Expedition member riding in wheeled vehicle," Bult said.

We turned around to look at him. He was standing beside his pony, talking into his log. "Disruption of land surface."

I got out of the rover and stalked over to him. "I told you, you can't fine somebody who's not a member of the expedition."

Bult looked at me. "Inappropriate tone and manner." He straightened some finger joints at me. "You member. Cahsson member. Yahhs?" he said in the maddening pidgin he uses when he's not tallying fines.

But his message was clear enough. If either of us rode back with Evelyn, he could fine us for using a rover, which would take the next six expeditions' wages, not to mention the trouble we'd get into with Big Brother.

"You expedition, yahhs?" Bult said. He held out his pony's reins to me.

"Yeah," I said. I took the reins.

Bult grabbed his log off his pony's saddlebone, jumped in the rover, and folded himself into a sitting position. "We go," he said to Evelyn.

Evelyn looked questioningly at me.

"Bult here'll ride in with you," I said. "We'll bring the ponies in."

"How on hell are we supposed to bring three ponies in when they'll only walk two abreast?" Carson said.

I ignored him. "See you back at King's X." I slapped the side of the rover.

"Go fahhst," Bult said. Ev started the rover up and waved and left us eating a cloud of dust.

"I'm beginning to think you're right about loaners, Fin," Carson said, coughing and smacking his hat against his leg. "They're nothing but trouble. And the males are the worst, especially after C.J. gets to 'em. We'll spend half the expedition listening to him talk about her, and the other half keeping him from labeling every gully in sight Crissa Canyon."

"Maybe," I said, squinting at the rover's dust, which seemed to be veering off to the right. "C.J. said Evelyn got in this morning."

"Which means she's had almost a whole day to give him her pitch," he said, taking hold of Bult's pony's reins. It balked and dug in its paws. "And she'll have at least another two hours to work her wiles before we get these ponies in."

"Maybe," I said, still watching the dust. "But I figure a presentable-looking male like Ev can jump just about any female he wants without having to do anything for it, and you notice he didn't stay at King's X with C.J. He came tearing out here to meet *us*. I think he might be smarter than he looks."

"That's what you said the first time you saw Bult," Carson said, yanking on Bult's pony's reins. The pony yanked back.

"And I was right, wasn't I?" I said, going over to help. "If he wasn't, he'd be here with these ponies, and *we'd* be halfway to King's X." I took over the reins, and he went around behind the pony to push.

"Maybe," he said. "Why wouldn't he want to meet us? After all, we're planetary surveyors. We're famous!"

I pulled and he pushed. The pony stayed put. "Get moving, you rock-headed nag!" Carson said, shoving on its back end. "Don't you know who we are?"

The pony lifted its tail and dumped a pile.

"My *shit*!" Carson said.

"Too bad Evelyn can't see us now," I said, holding the reins over my shoulder and hauling on the pony. "Findriddy and Carson, the famous explorers!"

Off in the distance, to the right of the ridge, the dust disappeared.

Interim: At King's X

It took us four hours to make it into King's X. Bult's pony keeled over twice and wouldn't get up, and when we got there, Ev was waiting out at the stable to ask us when we were going to start on the expedition. Carson gave him an inappropriate-in-tone-and-manner answer.

"I know you just got back and have to file your reports and everything," Ev said.

"And eat," Carson muttered, limping around his pony, "and sleep. And kill me a scout."

"It's just that I'm so excited to see Boohte," Ev said. "I still can't believe I'm really *here*, talking to—"

"I know, I know," I said, unloading the computer. "Findriddy and Carson, the famous surveyors."

"Where's Bult?" Carson asked, unstrapping his camera from his pony's saddlebone. "And why isn't he out here to unload his pony?"

Evelyn handed Carson Bult's log. "He said to tell you these are the fines from the trip in."

"He wasn't *on* the trip in," Carson said,

glaring at the log. "What on hell are these? 'Destruction of indigenous flora.' 'Damage to sand formations.' 'Pollution of atmosphere.' "

I grabbed the log away from Carson. "Did Bult give you directions back to King's X?"

"Yes," Ev said. "Did I do something wrong?"

"Wrong?!" Carson spluttered. "*Wrong?!*"

"Don't get in a sweat," I said. "Bult can't fine Ev till he's a member of the expedition."

"But I don't understand," Ev said. "What did I do wrong? All I did was drive the rover—"

"Stir up dust, make tire tracks," Carson said, "emit exhaust—"

"Wheeled vehicles aren't allowed off government property," I explained to Ev, who was looking amazed.

"Then how do you get around?" he asked.

"We don't," Carson said, glaring at Bult's pony, which looked like it was getting ready to keel over again. "Explain it to him, Fin."

I was too tired to explain anything, least of all Big Brother's notion of how to survey a planet. "You tell him about the fines while I go get this straightened out with Bult," I said, and went across the compound to the gate area.

In my log, there's nothing worse than working for a government with the guilts. All we were doing on Boohte was surveying the planet, but Big Brother didn't want anybody accusing them of "ruthless imperialist expansion" and riding roughshod over the indidges the way they did when they colonized America.

So they set up all these rules to "preserve planetary ecosystems" (which was supposed to mean we weren't allowed to build dams or kill the local fauna) and "protect indigenous cultures from technological contamination" (which was supposed to mean we couldn't give 'em firewater and guns), and stiff fines for breaking the rules.

Which is where they made their first mistake, because they paid the fines to the indidges, and Bult and his tribe knew a good thing when they saw it, and before you know it we're being fined for making footprints, and Bult's buying technological contamination right and left with the proceeds.

I figured he'd be in the gate area, up to his second knee joint in stuff he'd bought, and I was right. When I opened the door, he was prying open a crate of umbrellas.

"Bult, you can't charge us with fines the rover incurred," I said.

He pulled out an umbrella and examined it. It was the collapsible kind. He held the umbrella out in front of him and pushed a button. Lights came on around the rim. "Destruction of land surface," he said.

I held out his log to him. "You know the regs. 'The expedition is not responsible for violations committed by any person not an official member of the expedition.'"

He was still messing with the buttons. The lights went off. "Bult member," he said, and the umbrella shot out and open, barely missing my stomach.

"Watch it!" I jumped back. "You can't incur fines, Bult."

Bult put down the umbrella and opened a big box of dice, which would make Carson happy. His favorite occupation, next to blaming me, is shooting craps.

"Indidges can't incur fines!" I said.

"Inappropriate tone and manner," he said.

I was too tired for this, too, and I still had the reports and the whereabouts to do. I left him unpacking a box of shower curtains and went across to the mess.

I opened the door. "Honey, I'm home," I called.

"Hello!" C.J. sang out cheerfully from the kitchen, which was a switch. "How was your expedition?"

She appeared in the doorway, smiling and wiping her hands on a towel. She was all done up, clean face and fixed-up hair and a shirt that was open down to thirty degrees north. "Dinner's almost ready," she said brightly, and then stopped and looked around. "Where's Evelyn?"

"Out in the stable," I said, dumping my stuff on a chair, "talking to Carson, the planetary surveyor. Did you know we're famous?"

"You're filthy," she said. "And you're late. What on hell took you so long? Dinner's cold. I had it ready two hours ago." She jabbed a finger at my stuff. "Get that dirty pack off the furniture. It's bad enough putting up with dust tantrums without you two dragging in dirt."

I sat down and propped my legs up on the table. "And how was your day, sweetheart?" I said. "Get a mud puddle named after you? Jump any loners?"

"Very funny. Evelyn happens to be a very nice young man who understands what it's like to be all alone on a planet for weeks at a time with nobody for hundreds of kloms and who knows what dangers lurking out there—"

"Like losing that shirt," I said.

"You're not exactly in a position to criticize my clothes," she said. "When's the last time you changed *yours*? What have you been doing, rolling in the mud? And get those boots off the furniture. They're disgusting!" She smacked my legs with the dish towel.

This was as much fun as talking to Bult. If I was

going to be raked over the coals, it might as well be by the experts. I heaved myself out of the chair. "Any pursuants?"

"If you mean official reprimands, there are sixteen. They're on the computer." She went back to the kitchen, her shirt flapping. "And get cleaned up. You're not coming to the table looking like that."

"Yes, dear," I said and went over to the console. I fed in the expedition report and took a look at the subsurfaces I'd run in Sector 247-72, and then called up the pursuants.

There were the usual loving messages from Big Brother: we weren't covering enough sectors, we weren't giving enough f-and-f indigenous names, we were incurring too many fines.

"Pursuant to language used by members of survey expeditions, such members will refrain from using derogatory terms in reference to the government, in particular, abbreviations and slang terms such as 'Big Brother' and 'morons back home.' Such references imply lack of respect, thereby undermining relations with the indigenous sentients and obstructing the government's goals. Members of survey expeditions will henceforth refer to the government by its proper title in full."

Evelyn and Carson came in. "Anything interesting?" Carson asked, leaning over me.

"We're wearing our mikes turned up too high," I said.

He clapped me on the shoulder. "I'm gonna go check the weather and then take a bath," he said.

I nodded, looking at the screen. He left, and I started through the pursuants again and then looked back behind me. Ev was leaning over me, his chin practically on my shoulder.

"Do you mind if I watch?" he said. "It's so exc—"

"I know, I know," I said. "There's nothing more exciting then reading a bunch of memos from Big Brother. Oh. Sorry," I said, pointing at the screen, "we're not supposed to call them that. We're supposed to use appropriate titles. There's nothing more exciting than reading memos from the Third Reich."

Ev grinned, and I thought, Yep, smarter than he looks.

"Fin," C.J. called from the door of the mess. She'd unstripped her blouse another ten degrees. "Can I borrow Evelyn for a minute?"

"You bet, Crissa Jane," I said.

She glared at me.

"That's what C.J. stands for, you know," I said to Ev. "Crissa Jane Tull. You'll need to remember that for when we go on expedition."

"Fin!" she snapped. "Ev," she said sweetly, "can you come help me with dinner?"

"Sure," Ev said and was after her like a shot. All right, not that much smarter.

I went back to the pursuants. We weren't showing "proper respect for indigenous cultural integrity," which meant who knows what, we hadn't filled out Subsection 12-2 of the minerals report for Expedition 158, we had left two gaps of uncharted territory on Expedition 162, one in Sector 248-76 and the other in Sector 246-73.

I knew what the 246-73 gap was but not the other one, and I doubted if it was still a gap. We'd been over a lot of the same territory the next-to-last expedition.

I called up the topographicals and asked for a chart

overlay. Big Bro—Hizzoner was right for once. There were two holes in the chart.

Carson came in, carrying a towel and a clean pair of socks. "We fired yet?"

"Just about," I said. "How's the weather look?"

"Rain down in the Ponypiles start of next week. Otherwise, nothing. Not even a dust tantrum. Looks like we can go anywhere we want."

"What about in charted territory? Up along 76?"

"Same thing. Clear and dry. Why?" he said, coming over to look at the screen. "What've you got?"

"I don't know yet," I said. "Probably nothing. Go get cleaned up."

He went off toward the latrine. Sector 248-76. That was over on the other side of the Tongue and, if I remembered right, close to Silvershim Creek. I frowned at the screen a minute and then asked for Expedition 181's log and started fast-forwarding it.

"Is that the expedition you were just on?" Ev said, and I jerked around to find him hanging over me again.

"I thought you were helping C.J. in the kitchen," I said, cutting the log off.

He grinned. "It's too hot in there. Were you sending the log of the expedition to NASA?"

I shook my head. "The log goes out live. It transmits straight to C.J. and she sends it on through the gate. I was just finishing up the expedition summary."

"Do you send all the reports?"

"Nope. Carson sends the topographicals and the F-and-F; I send the geologicals and the accountings." I asked for the tally of Bult's fines.

Ev looked uneasy. "I wanted to apologize to you for driving the rover. I didn't know it was against regs to use nonindigenous transportation. The last thing I wanted to do on my first day was to get you and Dr. Carson in trouble."

"Don't worry about it. We still had wages left over this expedition, which is better than we've made out the last two. The only things that really get you in trouble are killing fauna and naming something after somebody," I said, staring at him, but he didn't look especially guilty. C.J. must not have gotten around to her sales pitch yet.

"Anyway," I said, "we're used to trouble."

"I know," he said earnestly. "Like the time you got caught in the stampede and nearly got trampled, and Dr. Carson rescued you."

"How'd you know about that?" I asked.

"Are you kidding? You're—"

"Famous. Right," I said. "But how—"

"Evelyn," C.J. called, dripping honey with every syllable, "can you help me set the table?" and he was off again.

I got 181's log again and then changed my mind and asked for the whereabouts. I checked them for the two times we'd been in Sector 248-76. Wulfmeier'd been on Starting Gate both times, which didn't prove anything. I asked for a verify on him.

"Nahhd khompt," Bult said.

I looked up. He was standing next to the computer, pointing his umbrella at me.

"I need the computer, too," I said, and he reached for his log. "Besides, it's almost dinnertime."

"Nahhd tchopp," he said, moving around behind me so he could see the screen. "Forcible confiscation of property."

"That's what it is, all right," I said, wondering which was worse, being stuck with his bayonet of an umbrella or another fine. Besides, I couldn't find out what I needed to know with all these people hanging over my shoulder. And dinner was ready. Evelyn pushed the kitchen door open with his shoulder and brought out a platter of meat. I asked for the catalog.

"Here you go," I said, standing up. "Nieman Marcus at your disposal. Go at it. Tchopp."

Bult sat down, shot his umbrella open, and started talking to the computer. "One dozen pair digiscan polarized field glasses," he said, "with telemetry and object enhancement functions."

Ev stared.

"One 'High Rollers Special' slot machine," Bult said.

Ev came over with the platter. "Bult can speak English?" he said.

I grabbed a chunk of meat. "Depends. When he's ordering stuff, yeah. When you're talking to him, not much. When you're trying to negotiate satellite surveys or permission to set up a gate, *no hablo inglais*." I grabbed another hunk of meat.

"*Stop* that!" C.J. said, bringing in the vegetables. "Honestly, Fin, you've got the manners of a gatecrasher! You could at least wait till we get to the table!" She set the vegetables down. "Carson! Dinner's ready!" she called and went back into the kitchen.

He came in, wiping his hands on a towel. He'd washed up and shaved around his mustache. He came over close to me. "Find anything?" he muttered.

"Maybe."

Ev, still holding the meat platter, was looking at me inquiringly.

I said, "I found out those binocs you lost are gonna cost us three hundred."

"*I* lost?" Carson said. "You're the one who lost 'em. I laid 'em right next to your pack. Why on hell's it three hundred?"

"Possible technological contamination," I said. "If they turn up on an indidge it'll be five hundred you lost us."

"*I* lost us!" he said.

C.J. came in, carrying a bowl of rice. She'd switched her shirt for one with even lower coordinates, and lights around the edges like the ones on Bult's umbrella.

"You were the one in a hurry to get back here and meet *Evelyn*," I said. I pulled a chair out from the table, stepped over it, and sat down.

He grabbed the platter out of Ev's hands. "Five hundred. My *shit*!" He set the platter on the table. "How much were the rest of the fines?"

"I don't know," I said. "I haven't tallied 'em yet."

"Well, what on hell were you doing all this time?" He sat down. "It's plain to see you weren't taking a bath."

"C.J.'s cleaned up enough for both of us," I said. "What're the lights for?" I asked her.

Carson grinned. "They're like those landing strip beacons, so you can find your way down."

C.J. ignored him. "You sit here by me, Evelyn."

He pulled out her chair, and she sat down, managing to lean over so we could all see the runway.

Ev sat down next to her. "I can't believe I'm actually eating dinner with Carson and Findriddy! Tell me about your expedition. I'll bet you had a lot of adventures."

"Well," Carson said, "Fin lost the binocs."

"Have you decided when we leave on the next expedition yet?" Ev asked.

Carson gave me a look. "Not yet," I said. "A few days, probably."

"Oh, good," C.J. crooned, leaning in Ev's direction. "That'll give us more time to get to know each other." She latched onto his arm.

"Is there anything I can do to help so we can leave sooner?" Ev said. "Loading the ponies or something? I'm just so eager to get started."

C.J. dropped his arm in disgust. "So you can spend three weeks sleeping on the ground and listening to these two?"

"Are you kidding?" he said. "I put in four years ago for the chance to go on an expedition with Carson and Findriddy! What's it like, being on the survey team with them?"

"What's it like?" She glared at us. "They're rude, they're dirty, they break every rule in the book, and don't let all their bickering fool you—they're just like *that*." She crossed one finger over another. "Nobody has a chance against the two of them."

"I know," Ev said. "On the pop-ups they—"

"What are these pop-ups?" I said. "Some kind of holo?"

"They're DHVs," Ev said, as if that explained everything. "There's a whole series of them about you and Carson and Bult." He stopped and looked around at Bult hunched over the computer under his umbrella. "Doesn't Bult eat with you?"

"He's not allowed to," Carson said, helping himself to the meat.

"Regs," I said. "Cultural contamination. Asking him to eat at a table and use silverware is imperialistic.

We might corrupt him with Earth foods and table manners."

"Small chance of that," C.J. said, taking the meat platter away from Carson. "You two don't *have* any table manners."

"So while we eat," Carson said, plopping potatoes on his plate, "he sits there ordering demitasse cups and place settings for twelve. Nobody ever said Big Brother was big on logic."

"Not Big Brother," I said, shaking my finger at Carson. "Pursuant to our latest reprimand, members of the expedition will henceforth refer to the government by its appropriate title."

"What, Idiots Incorporated?" Carson said. "What other brilliant orders did they come up with?"

"They want us to cover more territory. And they disallowed one of our names. Green Creek."

Carson looked up from his plate. "What on hell's wrong with Green Creek?"

"There's a senator named Green on the Ways and Means Committee. They couldn't prove any connection, though, so they just fined us the minimum."

"There're people named Hill and River, too," Carson said. "If one of them gets on the committee, what on hell do we do then?"

"I think it's ridiculous that you can't name things after people," C.J. said. "Don't you, Evelyn?"

"Why can't you?" Ev asked.

"Regs," I said. " 'Pursuant to the practice of naming geological formations, waterways, etc., after surveyors, government officials, historical personages, etc., said practice is indicative of oppressive colonialist attitudes and lack of respect for indigenous cultural traditions, etc., etc.' Hand the meat over."

C.J.'d picked up the platter, but she didn't pass it. "Oppressive! It is not. Why shouldn't we have something named after us? We're the ones stuck on this horrible planet all alone in uncharted territory for months at a time and with who knows what dangers lurking. We should get something."

Carson and I have heard this pitch a hundred or so times. She used to try it on us before she decided the loaners were more susceptible.

"There are hundreds of mountains and streams on Boohte. You can't tell me there isn't some way you could name *one* of them after somebody. I mean, the government wouldn't even notice."

Well, she's wrong there. Their Imperial Majesties check every single name, and even if all we tried to sneak past them was a bug named C.J., we could get tossed off Boohte.

"There's a way you can get something named after you, C.J.," Carson said. "Why didn't you say you were interested?"

C.J. narrowed her eyes. "How?"

"Remember Stewart? He was one of the first pair of scouts on Boohte," he explained to Ev. "Got caught in a flash flood and swept smack into a hill. Stewart's Hill, they named it. *In memoriam.* All you've got to do is take the heli out tomorrow and point it at whatever you want named after you, and—"

"Very funny," C.J. said. "I'm serious about this," she said to Ev. "Don't you think it's natural to want to have some sign that you've *been* here, so after you're gone you won't be forgotten, some monument to what you've done?"

"My *shit*," Carson said, "if you're talking about doing stuff, Fin and I are the ones who should have something named after us! How about it, Fin? You want me to name something after you?"

"What would I do with it? What I *want* is the meat!" I held out my hands for it, but nobody paid any attention.

"Findriddy Lake," Carson said. "Fin Mesa."

"Findriddy Swamp," C.J. said.

It was time to change the subject, or I was never going to get any meat. "So, Ev," I said. "You're a sexozoologist."

"Socioexozoologist," he said. "I study instinctive mating behaviors in extraterrestrial species. Courtship rituals and sexual behaviors."

"Well, you've come to the right place," Carson said. "C.J.—"

C.J. cut in, "Tell me about some of the interesting species you've studied."

"Well, they're all interesting, really. Most animal behaviors are instinctive, they're hardwired in, but reproductive behavior is really complicated. It's part hardwiring, part survival strategies, and the combination produces all these variables. The charlizards on Ottiyal mate inside the crater of an active volcano, and there's a Terran species, the bowerbird, which constructs an elaborate bower fifty times his size and then decorates it with orchids and berries to attract the female."

"Some nest," I said.

"Oh, but it's not the nest," Ev said. "The nest is built in front of the bower, and it's quite ordinary. The bower is just for courtship. Sentients are even more interesting. The Inkicce males cut off their toes to impress the female. And the Opantis' courtship ritual— they're the indigenous sentients on Jevo—takes six months. The Opanti female sets a series of difficult tasks the male must perform before she allows him to mate with her."

"Just like C.J.," I said. "What kind of tasks do these Opantis have to do for the females? Name rivers after them?"

"The tasks vary, but they're usually the giving of tokens of esteem, proofs of valor, feats of strength."

"How come the male's always the one who has to do all the courting?" Carson said. "Giving 'em candy and flowers, proving they're tough, building bowers while the female just sits there making up her mind."

"Because the male is concerned only with mating," Ev said. "The female is concerned with ensuring the optimum survival of her offspring, which means she needs a strong mate or a smart one. The male doesn't do all the courting, though. The females send out response signals to encourage and attract the males."

"Like landing lights?" I said.

C.J. glared at me.

"Without those signals, the courtship ritual breaks down and can't be completed," Ev said.

"I'll keep that in mind," Carson said. He pushed back from the table. "Fin, if we're gonna start in two days, we'd better take a look at the map. I'll go get the new topographicals." He went out.

C.J. cleared off the table, and I threw Bult off the computer and set up the map, filling in the two holes with extrapolated topographics before I went back over to the table.

Ev was bending over the map. "Is that the Wall?" he said, pointing at the Tongue.

"Nope. That's the Tongue. *That's* the Wall," I said,

sticking my hand in the middle of the holo to show him its course.

"I hadn't realized it was so long," he said wonderingly, tracing its meandering course along the Tongue and into the Ponypiles. "Which part is uncharted territory?"

"The blank part," I said, looking at the huge western expanse of the map. The charted area looked like a drop in the bucket.

Carson came back in and called Bult and his umbrella over, and we discussed routes.

"We haven't mapped any of the northern tributaries of the Tongue," Carson said, circling an area in light marker. "Where can we cross the Wall, Bult?"

Bult leaned over the table and pointed stiffly at two different places, making sure his finger didn't go into the holo.

"If we cross down here," I said, taking the marker away from Carson, "we can cut across here and follow Blacksand Ridge up." I lit a line up to Sector 248-76 and through the hole. "What do you think?"

Bult pointed at the other break in the Wall, holding his hinged finger well above the table. "Fahtsser wye."

I looked across at Carson. "What do you think?"

He looked steadily back at me.

"Will we get to see the trees that have the silver leaves?" Ev said.

"Maybe," Carson said, still looking at me. "Either way looks good to me," he said to Bult. "I'll have to check on the weather and see which one'll work. It looks like there's a lot of rain down here." He poked his finger at the route Bult'd marked. "And we'll have to run terrains. Fin, you want to do that?"

"You bet," I said.

"I'll check the weather, and see if we can work a route through some silvershims for Evie here."

He went out. "Can I watch you run the terrains?" Ev asked me.

"You bet," I said. I went over to the computer.

Bult was on it again, hunched under his umbrella, buying a roulette wheel.

"I've got to figure the easiest route," I said. "You can come back to the mall when I'm done."

He got out his log. "Discriminatory practices," he said.

That was a new one. "Why all these fines, Bult?" I said. "You saving up to buy a—" I was about to say "casino" but the last thing I wanted to do was give him any ideas. "To buy something big?" I ended up.

He reached for his log again.

"I need the computer if you want me to enter those fines you ran up with the rover today," I said.

He hesitated, wondering whether fining me for "attempt to bribe indigenous scout" would be worth more than the rover's fines, and then unfolded himself joint by joint and let me sit down.

I stared at the screen. There was no point in running terrains when I already knew the route I wanted, and I couldn't look at the log with Butt and Ev there either. I started tallying the fines.

After a few minutes C.J. came in and dragged Ev off to convince him Big Brother wouldn't catch him if he named one of the hills Mount C.J., but Bult was still hovering behind me, his umbrella aimed at my back.

"Don't you need to go unpack all those umbrellas and shower curtains you bought?" I said, but he didn't budge.

I had to wait till everybody was bedded down, including C.J., who'd flounced into her bunk in a hide-nothing nightie and then leaned out to say good night to Ev and give him one last eyeful, before I could take a look at that log.

I figured Bult would be in the gate area, unpacking his purchases, but he wasn't. Which meant he was still "tchopping," and I'd never get time alone on the computer. But he wasn't in the mess either.

I checked the kitchen and then started over to the stables. Halfway there I caught sight of a half circle of lights out by the ridge. I didn't have any notion of what he was doing clear out there—probably trying to collect fines from the luggage, but at least he wasn't hogging the computer.

I walked out far enough to make sure it was him and not just his umbrella and then went back into the mess and asked Starting Gate for a verify on Wulfmeier. I got it, which didn't mean anything either. Bult could make more selling fake verifies than he makes off us.

I asked for a trace, then checked on the rest of the gatecrashers. We had beacons on Miller and Abeyta, and Shoudamire was in the brig on the *Powell*, which left Karadjk and Redfox. They were out on the Arm.

The trace showed Wulfmeier on Dazil until yesterday afternoon. I thought about it, and then asked for the log and frame-by-frame coordinates and leaned back to watch it.

I'd been right. Sector 248-76 was next to the Wall, about twenty kloms down from where we'd crossed, an area of grayish igneous hills covered with knee-high scourbrush, which was probably the reason we'd skirted it.

I asked for an aerial. C.J.'d sideswiped 248-76 on

one of her trips home. I put privacies on and asked for visuals. It looked the way I remembered it—hills and scourbrush, a few roadkill. The visual said fine-grained schist with phyllosilicates all the way down. I asked for the earlier log. That expedition we were south of it. It was hills and scourbrush on that end, too.

The schist we'd found on Boohte wasn't gold-bearing, and there were no signs of salt or drainage anomalies, so it wasn't an anticline. And we'd had good reasons for missing it both times—the first time we'd been following the Wall, looking for a break, and the second time we were trying to avoid 246-73. I couldn't see any indications either time that Bult was avoiding it. Even if he was, it was probably because the ponies would balk at the steepness of the hills.

On the other hand, we'd gone right by it twice, and you could hide almost anything in those hills. Including a gate.

I erased my transactions, took the privacies off, and walked back to the bunkhouse to talk to Carson.

Ev was leaning against the door. He looked so sappy-eyed and relaxed I wondered if C.J.'d broken down and given him a jump. She used to and then tried to get the loaners to name something for her afterward, but half the time they forgot, and she decided it worked better the other way around. But I figured the way she was looking at him at dinner it was just possible.

"What are you doing out here?" I asked him.

"I couldn't sleep," he said, looking out in the direction of the ridge. "I still can't convince myself I'm really here. It's beautiful."

He had that right. All three of Boohte's moons were up, strung out in a row like an expedition and turning the ridge a purplish-blue. I leaned against the other side of the door.

"What's it like, out in uncharted territory?" he said.

"It's like those mating customs of yours," I said. "Part instinct, part survival strategies, way too many variables. Mostly, it's a lot of dust and triangulations," I said, even though I knew he wouldn't believe me. "And ponypiles."

"I can't wait," he said.

"Then you'd better be getting to bed," I said, but he didn't move.

"Did you know a lot of species perform their courtship rituals by moonlight?" he said. "Like the whippoorwill and the Antarrean cowfrog."

"And teenagers," I said, and yawned. "We'd better be getting to bed. We've got a lot to do in the morning."

"I don't think I could sleep," he said, still with that dopey look. I began to wonder if I'd been wrong about him being all that smart.

"I saw the vids, but they don't do it justice," he said, looking at me. "I had no idea everything would be so beautiful."

"You should be using that line on C.J. and her nightie," Carson said, poking his head around the door. He was wearing his liner and his boots. "What on hell's going on out here?"

"I was telling Ev how he'd better get to bed so we can start in the morning," I said, looking at Carson.

"Really?" Ev said. The sappy-eyed look disappeared. *"Tomorrow?"*

"Sunup," I said, "so you'd better get back to your bunk. It's the last chance you'll have at a mattress for two weeks," but he didn't show any signs of leaving, and I couldn't talk to Carson with him hanging over me.

"Where are we going?"

"Uncharted territory," I said. "But you'll be asleep in the saddlebone and miss it if you don't get to bed."

"Oh, I couldn't possibly sleep now!" he said, gazing out at the ridge. "I'm too excited!"

"You'd better pack your gear then," Carson said.

"I'm all packed."

C.J. came out, pulling a hide-nothing robe on over her nightie.

"We're leaving at sunup," I told her.

"Oh, but you can't go *yet*," she said and yanked Ev inside.

Carson motioned me out halfway between the bunkhouse and the stable. "What did you find?"

"A hole in Sector 248-76. We've missed it twice, and Bult was leading both times."

"Fossil strata?"

"No. Metamorphic. It's probably nothing, but Wulfmeier was on Dazil yesterday afternoon, *and* verified on Starting Gate. I don't think he's either place."

"What do you think he's doing? Mining?"

"Maybe. Or using it as headquarters while he looks around."

"Where'd you say it was?"

"Sector 248-76."

"My shit," he said softly. "That's awfully close to 246-73. If it is Wulfmeier, he's bound to find it. You're right. We'd better get out there." He shook his head. "I wish we weren't stuck taking this loaner with us. What was he doing out here? Resting between rounds with C.J.?"

"We were discussing mating customs," I said.

"Sexozoologist!" he said. "Sex can mess up an expedition quicker than anything."

"Ev can handle C.J. Besides, she's not going on the expedition."

"It's not C.J. I'm worried about."

"What *are* you worried about, then? Him trying to name one of the tributaries Crissa Creek? Him building a nest fifty times his size? What?"

"Never mind," he said and stomped off toward the gate area. "I'll tell Bult," he said. "You load the ponies."

Expedition 184: Day 1

We ended having C.J. fly us as far as the Tongue. Carson and I tallied up how long it would take to get to uncharted territory and how many fines we'd run up on the way and decided it was cheaper to go by heli, even with the airborne vehicle fines. And C.J. was overjoyed to have a few last chances at Ev. She kept him up front with her the whole way.

"Quit lollygagging with Evie and send him back here," Carson called to C.J. when the Tongue came in sight. "We've got to check his gear."

He came back into the bay immediately, looking as excited as a kid. "Are we in uncharted territory yet?" he asked, squatting down and looking out through the open hatch.

"We charted all this side of the river last time," I said. "The regs are no alcohol, no tobacco, no rec drugs, no caffeine. You carrying any of those?"

"No," he said.

I handed him his mike, and he stuck it on

his throat. "No advanced technology except for scientific equipment, no cameras, no lasers or firearms."

"I've got a knife. Can I take that?"

"Only if you don't kill anything indigenous with it," I said.

"If you get the urge to kill something, kill Fin," Carson said. "There's no fine on us."

The heli swooped down to the Tongue and hovered above the near shore. "You're the first out," I said, pushing him over to the door. "It's too big a fine to land," I shouted. "C.J.'s going to hover it. We'll throw down the gear to you."

He nodded and got ready to jump. Bult elbowed him aside, shot his umbrella open, and floated down like Mary Poppins.

"Second out," I shouted. "Don't land on any flora if you can help it."

He nodded again, looking down at Bult, who already had his log out.

"Wait!" C.J. said and came shooting out of her pilot's seat and past Ev and me. "I couldn't let you go without saying good-bye, Ev," she said, and flung her arms around his neck.

"What on hell are you doing, C.J.?" Carson said. "Do you know how big the fine is for crashing a heli?"

"It's on automatic," she said, and planted a wet one on Ev. "I'll be waiting," she said breathily. "Good luck, I hope you find lots of things to name."

"We're all waiting," I said. "All right, you told her good-bye, Ev. Now, jump."

"Don't forget," C.J. whispered, and leaned forward to kiss him again.

"Now," I said, and gave him a push. He jumped, and C.J. latched onto the edge of the bay and glared at me. I ignored her and started handing the bedrolls and the surveying equipment down to him.

"Don't set the terminal on any flora," I shouted down to him, too late. He'd already laid it in a patch of scourbrush.

I glanced at Bult, but he'd gone down to the river's edge and was looking at the other side with his binocs.

"Sorry," Ev shouted to me. He jerked the terminal back up and looked around for a bare spot.

"Stop gossiping and jump," Carson said behind me, "so I can get the ponies unloaded."

I grabbed the supply packs and handed them down to Ev. "Stand back," I shouted to him, scanning the ground for a clear patch.

"What on hell's keeping you?" Carson shouted. "They're going to unload before I unload them."

I picked a bare spot and jumped, but before I'd so much as hit, Carson yelled, "Lower, C.J.," and I nearly cracked my head on the heli when I straightened up.

"Lower!" Carson bellowed over his shoulder, and C.J. dipped the heli down. "Fin, take the reins, dammit. What on hell are you waiting for? Lead 'em off."

I grabbed for the dangling reins, which did about as much good as it always does, but Carson always thinks the ponies are gonna suddenly turn rational and jump off. They reared and shied and backed Carson against the side of the heli's bay, like always, and Carson said, like always, "You rock-headed morons, get off me!" which Bult entered in his log.

"Verbal abuse of indigenous fauna."

"You're gonna have to push 'em off," I said, like always, and climbed back on.

"Ev," I shouted down, "we're bringing this down

as far as it'll go. Signal C.J. when it touches the tops of the scourbrush."

C.J. circled the heli and came in lower. "Up a little," Evelyn said, gesturing with his hand. "Okay."

We were half a meter from the ground. "Let's try it one more time," Carson said, like always. "Take the reins."

I did. This time they squashed him against the back of C.J.'s seat.

"Goddammit, you shit-brained sonsabitches," he shouted, swatting at their hind ends. They backed against him some more.

I maneuvered around to Carson's side, and picked up a hind paw of the one that was standing on his bad foot. The pony went over like it'd been doped, and we dragged it to the edge of the bay and pushed it out. It landed with an "oof" and laid there.

Evelyn hurried over. "I think it's hurt," he said.

"Nope," I said. "Just sulking. Stand back."

We upended the other three and dumped them on top of the first one and jumped down.

"Shouldn't we do something?" Evelyn said, looking anxiously at the heap.

"Not till we're ready to go," Carson said, picking up his gear. "They can't shit in that position. Come on, Bult. Let's get packed."

Bult was still over by the Tongue, but he'd dropped his binocs and was squatting on the bank, peering into the centimeter-deep water.

"Bult!" I shouted, walking over to him.

He stood up and got out his log. "Disturbance of water surface," he said, pointing up at the hovering heli. "Generation of waves."

"There's not enough water for a wave," I said,

sticking my hand in it. "There's hardly enough to wet your finger."

"Introduction of foreign body into waterway," Bult said.

"Foreign—" I started and was drowned out by the heli. It flew over the Tongue, rippling the centimeter's worth of water, and came back around, skimming the bushes. C.J. swooped past us, blowing kisses.

"I know, I know," I said to Bult, "disturbance of waterway."

He stalked over to a clump of scourbrush, unfolded an arm under it, and came up with two wiry leaves and a shriveled berry. He held them out to me. "Destruction of crop," he said.

C.J. banked and turned, waving, and headed off northeast. I'd told her to swing over Sector 248-76 on her way home and try to get an aerial. I hoped she wasn't so busy flirting with Ev that she'd forget.

Ev was looking south at the mountains. "Is that the Wall?" he said.

"Nope. The Wall's off that direction," I said, pointing across the Tongue. "Those are the Ponypiles."

"Are we going there?" Ev said, looking sappy-eyed again.

"Not this trip. We'll follow the Tongue south a few kloms and then head northwest."

"Will you two stop sight-seeing and get over here and load these ponies?" Carson shouted. He had the ponies up and was strapping the wide-angle to Speedy's pommelbone.

"Yes, ma'am," I said. Ev and I picked our way over to him between grass clumps. "Don't worry about the Wall," I told Ev. "We'll see plenty of it. We have to cross it to get to where we're going, and after we do we'll follow it all the way north to Silvershim Creek."

"Not unless we get these ponies loaded," Carson said. "Here," he said, handing the reins of one of the ponies to Ev. "Get Cyclone loaded."

"Cyclone?" Ev said, looking warily at the pony, which looked to me like it was getting ready to fall over again.

"There's nothing to it," I said. "Ponies—"

"Fin's right," Carson said. "Just don't make any sudden movements. And if he tries to throw you, hang on for dear life, no matter what. Cyclone doesn't get violent except when he senses fear."

"Violent?" Ev said, looking nervous. "I haven't had much experience riding."

"You can ride mine," I said.

"Diablo?" Carson said. "You think that's a good idea after what happened before? No, I think you'd better ride Cyclone." He held out the stirrup. "You just put your foot in here and take hold of the pommelbone nice and slow," he said.

Ev took hold of the pommel like it was a hand grenade. "There, there, Cyclone," he murmured, bringing his foot up in slow motion to the stirrup. "Nice Cyclone."

Carson looked across at me, the edges of his mustache quaking. "Isn't he doing good, Fin?"

I ignored him and went on attaching the wide-angles to Useless's chest.

"Now swing your other leg up and over, real slow. I'll hold him till you're on," Carson said, holding on tight to the bridle. Evelyn did it and got a death grip on the reins.

"Giddyap!" Carson shouted and smacked the pony

on the flank. The pony took a step forward, and Ev dropped the reins and grabbed for the pommelbone. The pony took two more steps toward Carson, lifted its tail, and dumped a pile the size of Everest.

Carson came over to me, laughing fit to kill.

"What are you picking on Ev for?" I said.

He laughed awhile before he answered. "You said he was smarter than he looks. I was just checking it out."

"You should be checking out your scout," I said, pointing at Bult, who had his binocs up to his eyes again, "if you want to depart any time today."

He laughed some more and went over to talk to Bult. I finished attaching the surveying equipment. Bult had his log out, and from the looks of it Carson was yelling at him again.

I swung up onto Useless and rode over to where Ev was sitting on his pony. "Looks like we'll be here awhile," I said. "Sorry about Carson. It's his idea of a joke."

"I figured that out," he said. "Finally. What's his real name?" he said, gesturing at the pony. It took a step forward and stopped.

"Speedy," I said.

"And this is as fast as it goes."

"Sometimes it doesn't go this fast," I said.

Useless lifted its tail and unloaded.

"Tell me they don't do this all the time," Ev said.

"Not like this," I said. "Sometimes after we have 'em in the heli they get the runs."

"Great," he said. "I suppose sudden movements don't spook them?"

"Nothing spooks them," I said, "not even nibblers chewing on their toes. If they're scared or they don't want to do something, they just stand there and won't budge."

"What don't they like?"

"People riding them," I said. "Hills. They won't go up more than a two percent grade. Backtrailing over their own pawprints. Going more than two abreast. Going more than a klom an hour."

Ev was looking at me warily, like I was putting him on, too.

I held up my hand. "Scout's honor," I said.

"But you can walk faster than that," he said.

"Not when there's a fine for footprints."

He leaned sideways to look at Useless's paws. "But they leave footprints, don't they?"

"They're indigenous," I said.

"But how do you cover any territory?"

"We don't, and Big Bro yells at us," I said, looking over at the Tongue. Carson had given up yelling and was watching Bult talk into his log. "Speaking of which, I'd better fill you in on the rest of the regs. No personal holo or picture-taking, no souvenirs, no picking wildflowers, no killing of fauna."

"What if you're attacked?"

"Depends. If you think you can survive the heart attack you'll have when you see the fine and all the reports you'll have to fill out, go ahead. Letting it kill you might be easier."

He looked suspicious again.

"We probably won't run into anything dangerous where we're going," I said.

"What about nibblers?"

"They're farther north. Hardly any of the f-and-f are dangerous, and the indidges are peaceful. They'll rob you blind, but they won't hurt you. You wear your mike all the time." I reached over and took it off and stuck it back on lower down on his chest. "If you get separated, wait where you are. Don't go trying to find anybody. That's the surest way to get yourself killed."

"I thought you said the f-and-f weren't dangerous?"

"They're not. But we're going to be in uncharted territory. That means landslides, lightning, roadkill holes, flash floods. You can cut your hand on scourbrush and get blood poisoning, or get too far north and freeze to death."

"Or get caught in a luggage stampede."

I wondered how he knew about that. The pop-ups, whatever they were. "Or wander off and never be found again, which is what happened to Stewart's partner, Segura" I said. "And you won't even get a hill named after you. So you stay where you are, and after twenty-four hours you call C.J. and she'll come and get you."

He nodded. "I know."

I was going to have to find out what these pop-ups are. "You call C.J." I said, "and you let her worry about finding the rest of us. If you're injured and can't call, she'll know where you are by your mike."

I paused, trying to remember what else I should tell him. Carson was yelling at Bult again. I could hear him clear over by the ponies.

"No giving the indidges gifts," I said, "no teaching them how to make a wheel or build a cotton gin. If you figure out what sex Bult is, no fraternizing. No yelling at the indidges," I said, looking over at Carson.

He was coming this way, his mustache quivering again, but he didn't look like he was laughing this time.

"Bult says we can't cross here," he said. "He says there's no break in the Wall here."

"When we looked at the map, he said there was," I said.

"He says it's been repaired. He says we'll have to ride south to the other one. How far is it?"

"Ten kloms," I said.

"My shit, that'll take us all morning," he said, squinting off in the direction of the Wall. "He didn't say anything about it being repaired when we did the map. Call C.J. Maybe she got an aerial of it on her way home."

"She didn't," I said. Swinging north to Sector 248-76, she wouldn't have gotten any pictures of where we were going.

"Dammit," he said, taking his hat off, looking like he was going to throw it on the ground and then thinking the better of it. He looked at me and then stomped back toward the Tongue.

"You stay here," I said to Ev. I dismounted and caught up to Carson. "You think Bult's got it figured out?" I asked him as soon as we were out of Ev's earshot.

"Maybe," he said. "So what do we do?"

I shrugged. "Go south to the next break. It's no farther from the northern tributaries, and by that time we'll know if we have to check 248-76. I sent C.J. up there to do an aerial." I looked at Bult, who was still talking into his log. "Maybe he doesn't have it figured out. Maybe there are just more fines this way."

"Which is just what we need," he said glumly.

He was right. Our departure fines came to nine hundred, and it took a half hour to tally them up. Then it took Bult another half hour to get his pony loaded, decide he wanted his umbrella, unload everything to find it and load it again, and by that time Carson had used inappropriate manner and tone and thrown his hat on the ground, and we had to wait while Bult added those on.

It was ten o'clock before we finally got started, Bult leading off under his lighted umbrella, which he'd tied to his pony's pommelbone, Ev and I side by side, and Carson in the rear where he couldn't swear at Bult.

C.J.'d landed us at the top end of a little valley, and we followed it south, keeping close to the Tongue.

"You can't see much from here," I told Ev. "This really only goes another klom or so, and then you should get a better view of the Wall. And five kloms down it comes right up next to the Tongue."

"Why is it called the Tongue? Is that a translation of the Boohteri name for it?"

"The indidges don't have a name for it. Or half the stuff on this planet." I pointed at the mountains ahead of us. "Take the Ponypiles. Biggest natural formation on the whole continent, and they don't have a name for it, or most of the f-and-f. And when they do give stuff names, they don't make any sense. Their name for the luggage is *tssuhlkahttses*. It means Dead Soup. And Big Brother won't let us give things sensible names."

"Like the Tongue?" he said, grinning.

"It's long, it's pink, and it's hanging out like it's going 'aah' for a doctor. What else would you call it? That's not its name anyway. The Tongue's just what we call it. The name on the map's Conglomerate River, after the rocks it was flowing between up where we named it."

"An unofficial name," Ev said, half to himself.

"Won't work," I said. "We already named Tight-ass Canyon after C.J. She wants something named after her officially. Passed, approved, and on the topographicals."

"Oh," he said, and looked disappointed.

"What about that?" I said. "Any species besides homo sap have to carve a female's name on a tree to get a jump?"

"No," he said. "There's a species of water bird on Choom where the males build plaster dikes around the females that look a lot like the Wall."

Speaking of which, there it was. The valley had been climbing and opening out as we rode, and all of a sudden we were at the top of a rise and looking out across what looked like one of C.J.'s aerials.

It was flat all the way to the feet of the Ponypiles, with the Tongue slicing through it like a map boundary. Boohte's got as many oxides as Mars, and lots of cinnabar, so the plains are pink. There were mesas here and there off to the west, and a couple of cinder pyramids, and the blue of the distance turned them a nice lavender. And meandering around them and over the mesas, down to the Tongue and then away again, arched white and shining in the sun, was the Wall. At least Bult hadn't been lying about the break. The Wall marched unbrokenly as far as I could see.

"There she is," I said. I turned and looked at Ev. His mouth was hanging open.

"Hard to believe the Boohteri built it, isn't it?"

Ev nodded without closing his mouth.

"Carson and I have this theory that they didn't," I said. "We think some poor species of indidges who lived here before built it, and then Bult and his pals fined them out of it."

"It's beautiful," Ev, who hadn't heard me, said. "I had no idea it was so long."

"Six hundred kloms," I said. "And getting longer.

An average of two new chambers a year, according to C.J.'s aerials, not counting repaired breaks."

Which meant our theory didn't wash at all, but neither did the idea of the indidges doing all the work.

"It's even more beautiful than the pop-ups," Ev said, and I was going to ask him what exactly they were, but I didn't think he'd hear that either.

I remembered the first time I'd seen the Wall. I'd only been on Boohte a week. We'd spent the whole time struggling up a draw in pouring rain and I'd spent the whole time wondering how I'd let Carson talk me into this, and we came out on top of a mesa a lot higher than what we were now, and Carson said, "There she is. All yours."

Which got us a pursuant on incorrect imperialistic attitudes and how "Pursuant to proprietorship, planets are *not* owned."

I looked over at Ev. "You're right. It is presentable-looking."

Bult finished writing up his fines, and we started out across it. He was still keeping close to the Tongue, and after half a klom he got out his binocs, looked through them at the water, and shook his head, and we plodded on.

It was already after noon, and I thought about getting lunch out of my pack, but the ponies were starting to drag and Ev was intent on the Wall, which was close to the Tongue here, so I waited.

The Wall disappeared behind a low step-mesa for a hundred meters and then curved down almost to the Tongue, and Carson's pony apparently decided he'd gone far enough and stopped, swaying.

"Uh-oh," I said.

"What is it?" Ev said, dragging his eyes away from the Wall.

"Rest stop. Remember how I told you they're not dangerous?" I said, watching Carson, who'd gotten down off his pony and was standing clear. "Well, that's if they don't fall over with your legs under 'em. Think you can get down off him faster than you got on?"

"Yes," Ev said, jumping down and away like he expected Speedy to explode.

I tightened the straps on the computer, dismounted, and stepped back. Up ahead, Carson's pony had stopped swaying, and Carson had gone back up to it and was trying to untie the food packs.

Ev and I walked up and watched him struggle with the line. The pony dumped a pile practically on Carson's foot and started swaying again.

"Tim-berr," I said, and Carson jumped back. The pony took a couple of tottering steps forward and fell over, its legs out stiff at its side.

The pack was half under it, and Carson started yanking it out from under the motionless carcass. Bult unfolded himself and stepped decorously off his pony holding his umbrella, and the rest of the ponies went over like dominoes.

Ev went over to Carson and stood looking down on him. "Don't make any sudden movements," he said.

Carson stomped past me. "What are *you* laughing at?" he said.

We had lunch and incurred a few fines, but I didn't get a chance to talk to Carson alone. Bult stuck like glue to us, talking into his log, and Ev kept asking questions about the Wall.

"So they make the chambers one at a time," he said, looking across at it. We were on the wrong side of the Wall here, so all you could see were the back walls of the chambers, looking like they'd been plastered and painted a whitish-pink. "How do they build them?"

"We don't know. Nobody's ever seen them doing it," Carson said. "Or seen them doing anything worthwhile," he added darkly, watching Bult tallying up, "like finding us a way across it so we can get on with this expedition."

He went over to Bult and started talking to him in an inappropriate manner.

"And what *are* they?" Ev asked. "Dwellings?"

"And storerooms for all the stuff Bult buys, and landfills. Some of them are decorated, with flowers hanging in the opening and nibbler bones laid out in a design in front of the door. Most of them stand empty."

Carson stomped back, his mustache quaking. "He says we can't cross here either."

"The other break's been repaired, too?" I said.

"No. Now he says there's something in the water. *Tssi mitss.*"

I looked over at the Tongue. It was flowing over quartzite sand here and was clear as glass. "What's that?"

"Your guess is as good as mine. It translates as 'not there.' I asked him how much farther we have to go, and all he'll say is 'sahhth.' "

Sahhth apparently meant halfway to the Ponypiles because he didn't even glance at the Tongue again once we had the ponies up and moving, and he didn't even bother to lead. He motioned Ev and me ahead, and went back to ride with Carson.

Not that we could get lost. We'd charted all this territory before, and all we had to do was keep close to the Tongue. The Wall dipped away from the water and off toward a line of mesas, and we went up a hill through a herd of luggage, grazing on dirt, and came out at another Scenic Point.

The thing about these long vistas is that you're not going to see anything else for a while, and we'd already catalogued the f-and-f along here. There weren't any, anyway—a lot of luggage, some tinder grass, an occasional roadkill. I ran geological contours and double-checked the topographicals, and then, since Ev was busy gawking at the scenery, ran the whereabouts.

Wulfmeier was on Starting Gate after all. He'd been picked up by Big Brother for removing ore samples. So he wasn't in Sector 248-76, and we could've spent another day at King's X, eating C.J.'s cooking and catching up on reports.

Speaking of which, I figured I might as well finish them up now. I asked for Bult's purchase orders.

He must've worked fast while we were at King's X. He'd spent all his fines and then some. I wondered if that was why we were heading south, because he'd *tchopped* himself into a hole.

I went through the list, weeding out weapons and artificial building materials and trying to figure out what he was going to do with three dozen dictionaries and a chandelier.

"What are you doing?" Ev said, leaning across to look at the log.

"Screening out contraband," I said. "Bult's not allowed to order anything with weapon potential, which in his case should have included umbrellas. It's hard to catch everything."

He leaned farther across. "You're marking them 'out of stock.' "

"Yeah. If we tell him he can't order them, he fines

us for discrimination, and he hasn't figured out yet that he doesn't have to pay for out-of-stock items, which keeps him from ordering even more stuff."

He looked like he was going to keep asking questions, so I called up the topographical instead and said, "Tell me some more about these mating customs you're an expert on. Are there any species who give their girlfriends dictionaries?"

He grinned. "Not that I've run across so far. Gift-giving is a major part of a majority of species' courtship rituals, though, including *Homo sapiens*. Engagement rings, and the traditional candy and flowers."

"Mink coats. Condos. Islands in the Tobo Sea."

"There are several theories about its significance," Ev said. "Most zoologists think the bestowing of a gift proves the male's ability to obtain and defend territory. Some socioexozoologists believe gift-giving is a symbolic enactment of the sex act itself."

"Romantic," I said.

"One study found gift-giving triggered pheromones in the female, which in turn produced chemical changes in the male that led to the next phase of the courtship ritual. It's hardwired into the brain. Sexual instincts pretty much override rational thought."

Which is why females'll run off with the first male who smiles at them, I thought, and why C.J. had been acting like a idiot at the landing. Speaking of which, here she was calling on the transmitter. "Home Base to Findriddy. Come in, Fin."

"What is it?" I said, taking off my mike and moving it up so she could hear me.

"You got a reprimand," she said. " 'Pursuant to relations between members of the survey expedition and native planet dwellers. All members of the expedition will show respect for the ancient and noble cultures of indigenous sentients and will refrain from making terrocentric value judgments.' "

Which could have waited till we got back from the expedition. "What did you really call for, C.J.?" I asked. As if I didn't know.

"Is Evelyn there? Can I talk to him?"

"In a minute. Did you get a picture of that north-west section?"

There was a long pause before her answer came back. "I forgot."

"What do you mean, you forgot?"

"I had other things on my mind. The heli prop sounded funny."

"On hell it did. The only thing on your mind was jumping Ev."

"I don't know what you're so upset about," she said. "That whole area's charted, isn't it?"

"Here's Ev," I said. I patched her through and showed Ev the transmit button, and then looked back at Carson.

He'd want to know what I'd found out or hadn't found out, but he and Bult were too far back to shout at, and besides, I didn't want Bult figuring out why we'd picked the route we had.

If he hadn't already. We'd long since passed the second break in the Wall, and he didn't show any signs of crossing the Tongue.

"I'll try," Ev said earnestly into his mike. "I promise."

It's about time for a dust storm, I thought, looking at the sky. Carson usually likes to have one on the first day anyway, just in case something comes up where we need one, but he was deep in conversation with Bult, probably trying to talk him into crossing the Tongue.

"I miss you, too, C.J.," Ev said.

Nothing was stopping me from pointing the camera at a likely suspect and doing one myself, but there wasn't so much as a haze on the horizon. The Wall was only half a klom off along this stretch, and sometimes there are little kick-up breezes along it, but not today. The air was as still as a roadkill.

"Look!" Ev said, and I thought he was talking to C.J., but he said, "Fin, what's that?" and pointed at a shuttlewren that was flying toward us.

"*Tssillirah,*" I said. "We call them shuttlewrens."

"Why?" he said, watching the little bird fly over my head and back toward the other two ponies.

I didn't waste breath answering. The shuttlewren circled Carson's head and started back for us, flapping its stubby pinkish wings like it was about to wear out. It made two trips around Ev's hat and started back for Carson again.

"Oh," Ev said, turning around to see it making the circuit again, flapping for dear life. "How long can it keep that up?"

"A long time. We had one follow us for fifty kloms like that one time up by Turquoise Lake. Carson figured up it flew almost seven hundred kloms."

Ev started asking for stuff on his log. "What does the Boohteri name for them mean?" he asked me.

"Wide mud," I said, "and don't ask what that's supposed to mean. Maybe they build their nests out of mud. But there's no mud around here."

Or dust, I thought. I went back to thinking about dust storms. If Bult and Carson had been up ahead of us, I'd've taken my foot out of the stirrup and dragged it in the dirt to stir up some dust, but the way it was, Bult would catch me, and Ev would stop talking about shuttlewrens and ask what I was doing.

I looked back at Carson and waved, thinking maybe that would signal him to do something, but he was so busy talking to Bult I couldn't get his attention. The shuttlewren, on its tenth lap, skimmed the top of his hat, but that didn't get his attention either.

"Oh, look!" Ev said.

I turned back around. He was half up in the saddle, pointing off toward the Wall. I couldn't see what at, which meant neither could the scans.

"Where?" I said.

"Over there," he said, pointing.

I finally saw what he was looking at—a couch potato lying down behind a roundleaf bush and looking like a ponypile with fur.

I didn't think the scan had enough res to pick it up, but I said, "I don't see anything," to stall while I set the camera on a narrow focus to the far left of it, just in case.

"Over *there*," Ev said. "Is that—"

I cut him off before he could get more specific. "My shit!" I shouted. "Put the shield on. That's a . . ." and hit the disconnect.

"What is it?" Ev said, reaching for his knife. "Is it dangerous?"

"What?" I said, locking the disconnect in for twelve minutes.

"That!" Ev said, waving his hand in the direction of the couch potato. "That brown thing over there."

"Oh, *that*," I said. "That's a couch potato. It's not dangerous. Herbivore. Lies down most of the time, except to eat. I didn't notice it lying there." I set my watch alarm for ten minutes.

"Then what were you looking at?" he said, staring worriedly at the horizon.

"The weather," I said. "We get dust tantrums close to the Wall, and they play hob with the transmitter." I punched the transmitter's send three or four times and then held it down. "C.J., you there? Calling Home Base. Come in, Home Base." I shook my head. "It's out. I was afraid of that."

"I didn't see any dust," Ev said.

"They're only a meter or so wide," I said, "and nearly invisible unless they're in your line of sight." I hit a few more keys at random. "I better go tell Carson."

I yanked hard on the pony's reins and prodded it in the sides. "Carson," I called. "We got a problem."

Carson was still deep in conversation with Bult. I gave the pony another prod, and it gave me an evil look and started backing. At this rate, the dust storm'd be over before I even made it back there. I should've made it twenty minutes. "C.J., you there?" I said into the transmitter, just to make sure it was off, and got down off the pony.

"Hey, Carson," I yelled, "the transmitter's down." I walked back to his pony. "Wind's picking up," I said. "Looks like we're in for a dust tantrum."

"When?" he said, with a glance at Bult, who was busy digging for his log to fine me for being off Useless.

"Now," I said.

"How long do you think it'll last?"

"Awhile," I said, looking speculatively at the sky. "Twelve minutes, maybe twelve and a half."

"Rest stop," Carson called, and Bult leapt off his pony and stalked over to look at my footprints.

Carson walked off in the direction of the couch potato. I looked back at Ev. He was standing with his head up and his mouth open, watching the shuttlewren. I caught up with Carson, and we squatted so we wouldn't attract the attention of the shuttlewren.

"What's wrong?" he said.

"Nothing," I said. "I just thought we should have one dust storm before we crossed into uncharted territory."

"You could have waited, then," Carson said. "We're not crossing anytime soon."

"Why not? Is this break fixed, too?"

He shook his head. "*Tssi mitsse*, which means big *tssi mitss*, which I figure translates as he's going to see to it we don't get anywhere near Sector 248-76. What did you find out from C.J.? Did the aerial show anything?"

"She didn't get it. She was too busy batting her eyes at Ev and forgot."

"Forgot?!" he said. He stood up. "I told you he was going to louse up this expedition. I suppose you were too busy pointing out the sights to run whereabouts either."

I stood up and faced him. "What on hell's that supposed to mean?"

"It means you two've been so busy talking I figured you'd forgotten all about a little detail like what's going on in 248-76. What on hell's interesting enough to talk about all day long anyway?"

"Mating customs," I said.

"Mating customs," he said disgustedly. "That's why you didn't run whereabouts?"

"I did run them. Whatever's in that sector, it's not Wulfmeier. He's on Starting Gate, and he's under arrest. I got a verify."

Carson stared south at the Ponypiles. "Then what on hell's Bult up to?"

The shuttlewren changed course in midflap and started toward us. "I don't know," I said, taking off my hat and waving with it to keep it away. "Maybe the indidges have got a gold mine up there. Maybe they're secretly building Las Vegas with all the stuff Bult's ordered." The wren circled my head and made a pass at Carson. "Maybe Bult's just trying to run up our fines by taking us the long way around. Did he say how much farther we'd have to go before we could cross the Tongue?"

"Sahhth," Carson said, mimicking Bult holding his umbrella and pointing. "If we go much farther south, we'll be in the Ponypiles. Maybe he's going to lead us into the mountains and drown us in a flash flood."

"And then fine us for being foreign bodies in a waterway." My watch beeped. "Looks like it's starting to clear up," I said. I picked up a handful of dirt, and we started back for the ponies.

Bult met us halfway. "Taking of souvenirs," he said, pointing sternly at the dirt in my hand. "Disturbances of land surface. Destruction of indigenous flora."

"Better transmit all those right away," I said, "before you forget."

I went over to Ev's and my ponies, the shuttlewren tailing me. While Ev was watching it circle his head, I blew dirt off my hand onto the camera lens and then swung up and looked at my watch. A minute to go.

I messed with the transmitter a little and called to Carson, "I think I've got it fixed. Come on, Ev."

I messed some more for Ev's benefit, taking off a chip and snapping it back into place, but I didn't need to have bothered. He was still gawking at the shuttlewren.

"Is that shuttlewren a male?" he asked.

"Beats me. You're the expert on sex." I released the disconnect, counted to three, hit it again, and counted to five. "Calling Ki—" I said, and kicked it on again. "—ng's X, come in C.J."

"C.J. here," she said. "Where on hell did you go?"

"Nothing serious, C.J. Just a dust tantrum. We're too close to the Wall," I said. "Is the camera back on?"

"Yes. I don't see any dust."

"We just caught the edge of it. It lasted about a minute. I've been spending the rest of the time trying to get the transmitter up and running."

"It's funny," she said slowly, "how a minute's worth of dust could do so much damage."

"It's one of the chips. You know how sensitive they are."

"If they're so sensitive, how come all that dust from the rover didn't jam them?"

"The rover?" I said, looking around blankly like one might drive up.

"When Evelyn drove out to meet you yesterday. How come the transmitter didn't cut out then?"

Because I'd been too busy worrying about Wulfmeier and wrestling the binocs away from Bult to even think of it, I thought. I'd stood there coughing and choking in the rover's dust and it hadn't even crossed my mind. My shit, that was all we needed, for C.J. to catch on to our dust storms. "No accounting for technology," I said, knowing she was never going to buy it. "Transmitter's got a mind of its own."

Carson came up. "You talking to C.J.? Ask her if she's got an aerial of the Wall along here. I want to know where the breaks are."

"Sure," I said, and hit disconnect again. "We got a problem. C.J.'s asking questions about the dust storm. She wants to know why the transmitter didn't go out with all that dust from the rover."

"The rover?" he said, and I could see it dawn on him like it had on me. "What did you tell her?"

"That the transmitter's temperamental."

"She'll never buy that," he said, glaring at Ev, who was watching the shuttlewren start another lap. "I told you he'd cause trouble."

"It's not Ev's fault. We're the ones who didn't have sense enough to recognize a dust storm when we saw it. I'm going back on. What do I tell her?"

"That it's dust getting in the chip that does it," he said, stomping back to his pony, "not just dust in the air."

Which maybe would have worked, except two expeditions ago I'd told her it was dust in the air that did it.

"Come on, Ev," I said. He came over and got on his pony, still watching the shuttlewren. I took my finger off the disconnect. "—ase, come in, Home Base."

"Another dust storm?" C.J. said sarcastically.

"There must still be some dust in the chip," I said. "It keeps cutting out."

"How come the sound cuts out at the same time?" she said.

Because we're still wearing our mikes too high, I thought.

"It's funny," she went on. "While you were out, I took a look at the meteorologicals Carson ran before you left. They don't show any wind for that sector."

"No accounting for the weather either, especially this close to the Wall," I said. "Ev's right here. You want to talk to him?"

I patched him in before she could answer, thinking sex wasn't always such a bad thing on an expedition. It would take her mind off the dust anyway.

Bult and Carson rode in a wide circle around us to get in the lead again, and we followed, Ev still talking to C.J., which mostly consisted of listening and saying "yes" every once in a while, and "I promise." The shuttlewren followed us, too, making the circuit back and forth like a sheep dog.

"What kind of nests do the shuttlewrens have?" Ev asked.

"We've never seen them," I said. "What did C.J. have to say?"

"Not much. Their nests are probably in this area," he said, looking across the Tongue. The Wall was almost up next to the bank, and there were a few scourbrush in the narrow space between, but nothing that looked big enough to hide a nest. "The behavior they're exhibiting is either protective, in which case it's a female, or territorial, in which case it's a male. You say they've followed you for long distances. Have you ever been followed by more than one at a time?"

"No," I said. "Sometimes one'll fall away and another one'll take over, like they're working in shifts."

"That sounds like territorial behavior," he said, watching the shuttlewren make the turn past Bult. It was flying so low it brushed Bult's umbrella, and he looked up and then hunched over his fines again. "I don't suppose there's any way to get a specimen?"

"Not unless it has a coronary," I said, ducking as it skimmed my hat. "We've got holos. You can ask the memory."

He did, and spent the next ten minutes poring over them while I worried about C.J. We'd talked her into believing the transmitter could be taken out by a gust of dust that wouldn't even show on the log, and then I'd stood there yesterday and let the transmitter get totally smothered with it and hadn't even had the sense to disconnect.

And now that she was suspicious, she wouldn't let it go. She was probably checking all the logs for dust storms right now and comparing them to the meteorologicals.

Bult and Carson were looking in the water again. Bult shook his head.

"The staking out of territory is a courtship ritual," Ev said.

"Like gangs," I said.

"The male butterfish sweeps an area of ocean bottom clear of pebbles and shells for the female and then circles it constantly."

I looked at the shuttlewren, which was rounding Bult's umbrella again. Bult put down his log and collapsed the umbrella.

"The Mirgasazi on Yoan stake out a block of airspace. They're an interesting species. Some of the females have bright feathers, but they're not the ones the males are interested in."

The shuttlewren flapped past us and up to Bult and Carson again. It rounded the bend, and Bult shot his umbrella open. The shuttlewren fell in midflap, and

Bult stabbed it with the tip of the umbrella a couple of times.

"I knew I should have put umbrellas on the weapons list," I said.

"Can I have it?" Ev said. "To see if it's a male?"

Bult unfolded his arm, picked up the shuttlewren, and rode on, plucking the feathers off it. When we had half of them off, he stuck the shuttlewren in his mouth and bit it in half. He offered Carson half. Carson shook his head, and Bult crammed the whole thing in.

"Guess not," I said. I leaned down and got a feather and handed it to him.

He was watching Bult chew. "Shouldn't there be a fine for that?" he said.

" 'All members of the expedition shall refrain from making value judgments regarding the indigenous sentients' ancient and noble culture,' " I said.

I picked up the pieces Bult spit out, which didn't amount to much, and gave 'em to Ev. And looked off at the horizon.

The Wall curved back away from the Tongue and out across the plain in a straight line. Beyond it there was a scattering of scourbrush and trees. There wasn't any wind, the leaves were hanging limp. What we needed was a good dust storm to throw C.J. off, but there wasn't so much as a breeze.

It wasn't C.J.'s figuring the dust storms out that worried me. She'd try to blackmail us into naming something after her, but she'd been doing that for years. But I didn't want her talking about it over the transmitter for Big Brother to hear. If they started looking at the log, they'd be able to see for themselves. There was no way there'd been a dust tantrum in this weather. There wasn't even any air. The feathers Bult was spitting out up ahead fell straight down.

Half a klom later we ran into a dust tantrum that was more like a full-blown rage. It got in the transmitter (but not before we'd gotten a full five minutes of it on the log), and up our noses and down our throats, and made it so dark we had to navigate by following the lights on Bult's umbrella.

By the time we got clear of it, it was getting dark for real, and Bult started looking for a good place to camp, which meant someplace knee-deep in flora so he could get the maximum in fines out of us. Carson wanted to get across the Tongue first, but Bult peered solemnly into the water and pronounced *tssi mitsse*, and while Carson was yelling, "Where? I don't see a damn thing!" the ponies started to sway, so we camped where we were.

We set up camp in a hurry, first because we didn't want to have to unload the ponies after they were down, and then because we didn't want to be stumbling around in the dark, but all three of Boohte's moons were up before we got the transmitter unloaded.

Carson went off to tie the ponies up downwind, and Ev helped me spread out the bedrolls.

"Are we in uncharted territory?" he asked.

"Nope," I said, shaking the dust out of my bedroll. "Unless you count what's on us." I spread the bedroll out, making sure it wasn't on any flora. "Speaking of which, I'd better go call C.J. and tell her where we are." I handed Carson's bedroll to him and started over to the transmitter.

"Wait," he said.

I stopped and turned back to look at him.

"When I talked to C.J., she wanted to know why the dust tantrum hadn't shown up on the log."

"And what did you tell her?"

"I said it came in at an angle and blindsided us. I said it blew up so fast I didn't even see it till you shouted, and by that time we were in the middle of it."

I *told* Carson he was smarter than he looked, I thought.

"How come you did that?" I said. "C.J.'d probably give you a free jump for telling her we blew up that storm ourselves."

"Are you kidding?" he said, looking so surprised I was sorry I'd said it. Of course he wouldn't betray us. We were Findriddy and Carson, the famous explorers who could do no wrong, even if he'd just caught us redhanded.

"Well, thanks," I said and wondered exactly how smart he was and what explanation I could get away with. "Carson and I had things we needed to discuss, and we didn't want Big Brother listening."

"It's a gatecrasher, isn't it? That's why the expedition left in such a hurry and why you keep running whereabouts when there isn't supposed to be anybody but us on the planet. You think somebody's illegally opened a gate. Is that why Bult's leading us south, to try to keep us from catching him?"

"I don't know what Bult's doing," I said. "He could have kept us away from a gatecrasher by crossing where we were this morning and leading us up along the Wall past Silvershim Creek. He didn't have to drag us clear down here. Besides," I said, looking at Bult, who was down by the Tongue with Carson and the ponies, "he doesn't like Wulfmeier. Why would he try to protect him?"

"Wulfmeier?" Ev said, sounding excited. "Is that who it is?"

"You know Wulfmeier?"

"Of course. From the pop-ups," he said.

Well, I should have known.

"What do you think he's doing?" Ev said. "Trading with the indigenous sentients? Mining?"

"I don't think he's doing anything. I got a verify this morning that he's on Starting Gate."

"Oh," he said, disappointed. In the pop-ups we must have gone after gatecrashers with lasers blasting. "But you want to go there just to make sure?"

"If Bult ever lets us cross the Tongue," I said.

Carson came stomping up. "I ask Bult if it's safe to water the ponies, and he pretends to look in the water and says, '*tssi mitss* nah,' so I say, 'Well, fine, since there aren't any *tssi mitss*, we can cross first thing in the morning,' and he hands me a pair of dice and says, 'Sahthh. Brik lilla fahr.'" He squatted down and rummaged in his pack. "My shit, 'lilla fahr' is practically in the Ponypiles." He glared at the mountains. "What on hell is he up to? And don't give me that stuff about fines." He pulled out the water analysis kit and straightened up. "He's got enough already to buy himself a different planet. Fin, did you get that aerial of the Wall from C.J. yet?"

"I was just calling her," I said. He stomped off, and I went over to the transmitter.

"What can I do?" Ev said, tagging after me like a shuttlewren. "Should I gather some wood for a fire?"

I looked at him.

"Don't tell me," he said, catching my expression. "There's a fine for gathering wood."

"And starting a fire with advanced technology, and

burning indigenous flora," I said. "We usually try to wait till Bult gets cold and builds one."

Bult didn't show any signs of getting cold, even though the wind over the Ponypiles that had sent that dust tantrum into us had a chill to it, and after supper he gave Carson some more dice and then went off and sat under his umbrella out by the ponies.

"What on hell's he doing now?" Carson said.

"He probably went to get the battery-powered heater he bought last expedition," I said, rubbing my hands together. "Tell us some more about mating customs, Ev. Maybe a little sex'll warm us up."

"Speaking of which, Evie, have you figured out which brand Bult is yet?" Carson said.

As near as I could tell, Ev hadn't so much as looked at Bult since we started, except when Bult was snacking on the shuttlewren, but he spoke right up.

"Male," he said.

"How do you figure that?" Carson said, and I was wondering, too. If it was table manners he was going by, that wasn't any sign. Every indidge I'd seen ate like that, and most of them didn't bother about taking the feathers off first.

"His acquisitive behavior," Ev said. "Collecting and hoarding property is a typical male courtship behavior."

"I thought collecting stuff was a female behavior," I said. "What about all those diamonds and monograms?"

"Gifts the male gives to the female are symbols of the male's ability to amass and defend wealth or territory," Ev said. "By collecting fines and purchasing manufactured goods, Bult is demonstrating his ability to gain access to the resources necessary for survival."

"Shower curtains?" I said.

"Utility isn't the issue. The male burin fish collects large quantities of black rock clams, which are of no practical value, since the burin fish only eats flora, and piles them into towers as part of the courtship ritual."

"And that impresses the female?" I said.

"Ability to amass wealth is indicative of the genetic superiority of the male, and therefore the increased chance of survival for her offspring. Of course she's impressed. There are other qualities that impress her, too. Size, strength, the ability to defend territory, like that shuttlewren we saw this afternoon—"

Which the female shuttlewrens probably hadn't been very impressed with, I thought.

"—virility, youth—"

Carson said, "You mean we're here freezing our hind ends off because Bult's trying to impress some *female*?" He stood up. "I told you sex can louse up an expedition faster than anything else." He grabbed up the lantern. "I'm not gonna end up with frostbite just because Bult wants to show his genes to some damn female."

He went stomping off into the dark, and I watched the bobbing lantern, wondering what had gotten into him all of a sudden and why Bult wasn't following him with his log if what Ev said was true. Bult was still sitting out by the ponies—I could see the lights on his umbrella.

"The indigenous sentients on Prii built bonfires as part of their courtship ritual," Ev said, rubbing his hands together to warm them. "They're extinct. They burned down every forest on Prii in less than five hundred years time." He tipped his head back and looked at the sky. "I still can't believe how beautiful everything is."

It was presentable-looking. There were a bunch of stars, and the three moons were jostling for position in the middle of the sky. But my teeth were chattering, and there was a strong whiff of ponypile from downwind.

"What are the names of the moons?" he said.

"Larry, Curly, and Moe," I said.

"No, really. What are the Boohteri names?"

"They don't have names for them. Don't get any idea of naming one after C.J., though. They're Satellite One, Two, and Three until Big Brother surveys them, which it won't anytime soon since the Boohteri won't agree to satellite surveys."

"C.J.?" he said, like he'd forgotten who she was. "They don't look anything like they did on the pop-ups. Nothing on Boohte has, except you. You look exactly like I thought you would."

"These pop-ups you're always talking about? What are they? Holo books?"

"DHVs." He got up, went over to this bedroll, and squatted down to get something out from under it. He came back, holding a flat square the size of a playing card, and sat down beside me.

"See?" he said and opened the flat card up like a book. "Episode Six," he said.

Pop-ups was a good name for them. The picture seemed to jump out of the middle of the card and into the space between us, like the map back at King's X, only this was full-size and the people were moving and talking.

There was a presentable-looking female standing next to a horse made up to be a pony and a squatty pink thing like a cross between an accordion and a fireplug. They were having an argument.

"He's been gone too long," the female said. She had on tight pants and a low-slung shirt, and her hair was long and shiny. "I'm going to go find him."

"It's been nearly twenty hours," the accordion said. "We must report in to Home Base."

"I'm not leaving here without him," the female said, and swung up on the horse and galloped away.

"Wait!" the accordion shouted. "You can't! It's too dangerous!"

"Who's that supposed to be?" I said, sticking my finger into the accordion.

"Stop," Ev said, and the scene froze. "That's Bult."

"Where's his log?" I said.

"I told you things were different from what I'd expected," he said, sounding embarrassed. "Go back."

There was a flicker, and we were back at the beginning of the scene.

"He's been gone too long!" Tight Pants said.

"If that's Bult, then who's that supposed to be?" I said.

"You," he said, sounding surprised.

"Where's Carson?" I said.

"In the next scene."

There was another flicker, and we were at the foot of a cliff, with big, fake-looking boulders all around. Carson was sitting at the bottom of the cliff, sprawled out against one of the boulders with a big gash in the side of his head and a fancy mustache that curled at the ends. Carson's mustache had never looked that good, not even the first time I saw him, and they had the nibblers all wrong, too—they looked like guinea pigs with false teeth—but what they were doing to Carson's foot was pretty realistic. I hoped they got to the part where I found him pretty soon.

"Next scene," I said, and it flickered to me coming straight down the cliff in those tight pants, blasting at the nibblers with a laser.

Which wasn't the way it happened at all. Unless I'd wanted to go down the same way Carson did, there was no way off the cliff. The nibblers had run off when I yelled, but I'd had to go back along the cliff till I came to a chimney and work my way down and back around, and it took three hours. The nibblers had run off again when they heard me coming, but they hadn't been gone long.

Tight Pants jumped the last ten feet and knelt down beside Carson, and started tearing strips she couldn't afford to lose off her shirt and tying them around Carson's foot, which only looked a little bloody around the toes, sobbing her eyes out.

"I didn't cry," I said. "You got any others?"

"Episode Eleven," Ev said, and the cliff flicked into a silvershim grove. Tight Pants and Fancy Mustache were surveying the grove with an old-fashioned transit and sextant, and the accordion was writing down the measurements.

It looked like somebody'd cut up pieces of aluminum foil and hung them on a dead branch, and Carson was wearing a blue fuzzy vest that I had a feeling was supposed to be luggage fur.

"Findriddy!" the accordion said, looking up sharply. "I hear someone coming!"

"What are you two doing?" Carson said and walked right into a silvershim. He looked around, his arms full of sticks. "What on *hell* is this?"

"You and me," I said.

"A pop-up," Ev said.

"Turn it off!" Carson said, and the other Carson and Tight Pants and the silvershims compressed into a black nothing. "What on hell's the matter with you, bringing advanced technology on an expedition? Fin, you were supposed to see to it he followed the regs!" He dumped the sticks with a clatter onto where the accordion'd been standing. "Do you know how big a fine Bult could slap us with for that?"

"I . . . I didn't know . . ." Ev was stammering, stooping down to pick up the pop-up before Carson stepped on it. "It never occurred to me . . ."

"It's no more advanced than Bult's binocs," I said, "or half the stuff he's ordered. And even if it was, he doesn't know anything about it. He's over there tallying up his fines." I pointed off toward the lights of his umbrella.

"How do you know he doesn't know? You can see it for kloms!"

"And you can hear you twice as far!" I said. "The only way he's going to find out about it is if he comes over to see what all the hollering's about!"

Carson snatched the pop-up away from Ev. "What else did you bring?" he shouted, but softer. "A nuclear reactor? A gate?"

"Just another disk," Ev said. "For the pop-up." He pulled a black coin out of his pocket and handed it to Carson.

"What on hell's this?" he said, turning it over.

"It's us," I said. "Findriddy and Carson, Planetary Explorers, and Our Faithful Scout, Bult. Thirteen episodes."

"Eighty," Ev said. "There are forty on each disk, but I only brought my favorites."

"You gotta see 'em, Carson," I said. "Especially your mustache. Ev, is there some way you can tone down the production so we can watch without letting the rest of the neighborhood in on it?"

"Yeah," Ev said. "You just—"

"Nobody's watching anything till we get a fire built and I make sure Bult's out there under that umbrella," he said, and stomped off for about the fourth time.

I got the sticks made into a passable fire by the time he got back, looking mad, which meant Bult *was* there.

"All right," he said, handing the pop-up back to Ev. "Let's see these famous explorers. But keep it down."

"Episode Two," Ev said, laying it on the ground in front of us. "Reduce fifty percent and cloak," and the scene came up, smaller and in a little box this time. Fancy Mustache and Tight Pants were clambering over a break in the Wall. Carson was wearing his blue fuzzy vest.

"You're the one with the fancy mustache," I said, pointing.

"Do you have any idea what kind of fine we'd get for killing a suitcase?" he said. He pointed at Tight Pants. "Who's the female?"

"That's Fin," Ev said.

"Fin?!" Carson said, and let out a whoop. "Fin?! Can't be. Look at her. She's way too clean. And she looks too much like a female. Half the time with Fin you can't even tell!" He whooped again and slapped his leg. "And look at that chest. You sure that's not C.J.?"

I reached out and slapped the pop-up shut.

"What'd you do that for?" Carson said, holding his middle.

"Time to turn in," I said. I turned to Ev. "I'm

gonna keep this in my boot tonight so Bult can't get hold of it," I said and went over to my bedroll.

Bult was standing next to Carson's bedroll. I glanced out toward the Tongue. The umbrella was still there, burning brightly.

Bult picked up my bedroll to look under it. "Damage to flora," he said, pointing at the dirt underneath.

"Oh, shut up," I said and crawled in.

"Inappropriate tone and manner," he said, and went back out toward his umbrella.

Carson laughed himself sick for another hour, and I lay there after that an hour or so waiting for them to go to sleep and watching the moons jostling for positions in the sky. Then I got the pop-up out of my boot and opened it on the ground beside me.

"Episode Eight. Reduce eighty percent and cloak," I whispered and lay there and watched Carson and me sitting on horses in a pouring rain and tried to figure out which expedition this was supposed to be. There was a blue buffalo standing up the hill from where we were, and the accordion was pointing at it. "It is called *soolkases* in the Boohteri tongue," he said, and I knew which one this was, only that wasn't the way it happened.

It had taken us four hours to figure out what Bult was saying. "*Tssilkrothes?*" I remembered Carson shouting.

"*Tssuhhtkhahckes!*" Bult had shouted back.

"Suitcases?!" Carson said, so mad his mustache looked like it'd shake off. "We can't name them suitcases!" and right then a couple thousand suitcases had come roaring up over the hill at us. My pony stood there like an idiot and nearly got both of us trampled.

In the pop-up verson my pony ran off, and I was

the one who stood there looking dumb till Carson galloped up and swung me up behind him. I was wearing high-heeled boots and pants so tight it was no wonder I couldn't run, and Carson was right, she was way too clean, but he hadn't had to fall in the fire laughing about it.

Carson swung me up, and we rode off, my tight pants hugging the horse and my hair streaming out behind me.

"Nothing here's what I expected," Ev had said back at King's X, "except you." Tonight he'd said, "You looked exactly the way I pictured you." Which, I thought, trying to figure out how to make the pop-up run it again, was pretty damn good.

Expedition 184: Day 2

By noon the next day we were still on this side of the Tongue and still heading south, and Carson was in such a foul mood I steered clear of him.

"Is he always this irritable?" Ev asked me.

"Only when he's worried," I said.

Speaking of which, I was getting a little worried myself.

Carson's water analysis hadn't showed up anything but the usual f-and-f, but Bult had insisted there were *tssi mitss* and led us south to a tributary. There were *tssi mitss* in the tributary, too, and he led us east along it till we came to one of its tributaries. This one didn't have any *tssi mitss*, but it zigzagged down through a draw too steep for the ponies, so Bult led us north along it, looking for a place to cross. At this rate we'd be back at King's X by suppertime.

But that wasn't what was worrying me. What was worrying me was Bult. He hadn't fined us for anything all morning, not even when we broke camp, and he kept looking off to the

south through his binocs. Not only that, but Carson's
binocs had turned up. He found them in his bedroll after breakfast.

"Fin!" he'd shouted, dangling them by the strap. "I
knew you had 'em. Where'd you find 'em, in your
pack?"

"I haven't seen 'em since the morning we left for
King's X when you borrowed 'em," I said. "Bult must've
had 'em."

"Bult? Why would he've taken 'em?" he said and
gestured at Bult, who was peering through his own
binocs at the Ponypiles.

I didn't know, which was what was worrying me.
The indidges don't steal, at least that's what Big Brother
tells us in the pursuants, and in all the expeditions we'd
gone on, Bult hadn't ever taken anything away from us
but our hard-earned wages. I wondered what else he
might start doing—like take us deep into uncharted territory and then steal our packs and the ponies. Or lead
us into an ambush.

I wanted to talk about it with Carson, but I
couldn't get close to him, and I didn't want to risk another dust storm. I tried riding up alongside him, but
Bult kept his pony dead even with Carson's and glared
at me when I tried to move up.

Ev stuck almost as close to me, asking questions
about the shuttlewren and telling me about appetizing
mating customs, like the male hanging fly, which spins
a big balloon of spit and slobber for the female to mess
with while he jumps her.

We finally found a place to cross the creek as it
zagged sideways across a momentarily flat space, and
headed southwest through a series of low hills, and I
did a triangulation and then started running terrains.

"Well, we're in uncharted territory now," I told Ev. "You can start looking around for stuff to name after C.J. so you can get your jump."

"If I wanted a jump, I could get it without that," he said, and I thought, I bet you could.

"I know how C.J. feels, though," he said, looking out across the plain. "Wanting to leave some mark. You go through that gate, and you realize how big a planet is, and how insignificant you are. You could be here your whole life and never even leave a footprint."

"Try telling that to Bult," I said.

He grinned. "Okay, maybe footprints. But nothing lasting. That's why I wanted to come on this expedition. I wanted to do something that would make me famous, like you and Carson. I wanted to discover something that would get me on the pop-ups."

"Speaking of which," I said, leaning down to pick up a rock, "how did we get on them?" I stuck the rock in my pack. "How'd they find out about the suitcases? And Carson's foot?"

"I don't know," Ev said slowly, as if the question hadn't ever occurred to him. "Your logs, I guess."

It hadn't been in the logs about my finding Carson right when the twenty-four hours were up, though. We'd told some of the stories to loaners, and one of the female ones had kept a diary. But Carson wouldn't have told her about my crying over him.

The hills through here were covered with scraggly plants. I took a holo of them and then halted Useless, which didn't take much, and dismounted.

"What are you doing?" Ev asked.

"Collecting pieces of the planet for you to leave C.J.'s mark on," I said, digging around the roots of a couple of the plants and sticking them in a plastic bag.

I picked up two more rocks and handed them to him. "Either of these look like a C.J. to you?"

I got back on, watching Bult. He hadn't even noticed I was off my pony, let alone reached for his log. He was peering through his binocs at the hills beyond the tributary.

"Don't you ever wish you could have something named after you, Fin?" Ev was asking.

"Me? Why on hell would I want that? Who the hell remembers who Bryce Canyon or Harper's Ferry are named after even when they've got their names on them? Besides, you can't name a thing just by putting it on a topographical map. That's not the way it works." I gestured at the Ponypiles. "When people get here, they won't call those the Findriddy Mountains. They'll call 'em the Ponypiles. People name things after what they look like, or what happened there, or what the indidge name sounds like, not according to regs."

"People?" Ev said. "You mean gatecrashers?"

"Gatecrashers," I said, "and miners and settlers and shopping mall owners."

"But what about the regs?" Ev said, looking shocked. "They're supposed to protect the natural ecology and the sovereignty of the indigenous culture."

I nodded my head at Bult. "And you think the indigenous culture wouldn't sell them the whole place for some pop-ups and a couple of dozen shower curtains? You think Big Brother's paying us to survey all this for his health? You think as soon as we find something they want, they won't be down here, regs or no regs?"

Ev looked unhappy. "Like tourists," he said. "Everybody's seen the silvershims and the Wall on the pop-ups, and they all want to come see them."

"And take holos of themselves being fined," I said,

even though I hadn't really thought of Boohte as a tourist attraction. "And Bult can sell them dried ponypiles for souvenirs."

"I'm glad I came before the rush," he said, looking at the water ahead. The hills parted on either side of the tributary, and it wouldn't matter whether there were *tssi mitss* or not. A wide sandbar stretched almost the full width of the water.

The ponies picked their way across it like it was quicksand, and Ev just about fell off, trying to lean down to look at it. "The female willowback needs to lay her eggs in still water, so the courtship ritual involves the male doing a swimming dance that dams up sand across the stream."

"And that's what this is?" I said.

"I don't think so. It looks like it's just a sandbar." He sat up in the saddlebone. "The female shale-dwelling lizard scratches a design in the dirt, and then the male scratches the same design on the shale."

I wasn't paying any attention. Bult was peering through the binocs at the hills between us and the Tongue, and Carson's pony was starting to sway. "Here's your big chance, Ev," I said. "Rest stop!"

After Carson and I did the topographicals and we had lunch, I hauled out my rocks and plastic bags and Carson emptied his bug-catcher, and we settled down to naming.

Carson started with the bugs. "Do you have a name for it?" he asked Bult, holding it away from Bult so he couldn't stuff it in his mouth, but Bult didn't even look interested.

He looked at Carson for a minute like he was thinking of something else, and then said what sounded to me like steam hissing and then metal being dragged over granite.

"*Tssimrrah?*" Carson said.

"*Thssahggih,*" Bult said.

"This'll take a while," I said to Ev.

Figuring out the indidge name for a thing isn't so much about understanding what Bult says as trying to keep it from all sounding the same. f-and-f all sounds like steam escaping in a blizzard, lakes and rivers sound like a gate opening, and rocks all begin with a belching "B," which makes you wonder about the indidges' opinion of Bult. All of them sound more or less the same, and none of them sound like English letters, which is a good thing, or everything would have the same name.

"*Thssahggah?*" Carson said.

"*Shhoomrrrah,*" Bult said.

I glanced at Ev, who was looking at the rocks and the bagged plants. It was fairly slim pickings—the only rock that didn't look like mud warmed over was horneblende, and the only flower had five ragged-looking petals, but I didn't think Ev would try what the loaners usually did, anyway, which was try to name the first flower we found a chrysanthemum, no matter what it looked like. Chrysa, for short.

Carson and Bult finally agreed on *tssahggah* for the bug, and I took holos of it and of the piece of horneblende and transmitted them and their names.

Bult had the flower, and was shaking his head.

"The indidges don't have a name for it," Carson said, looking at Ev. "How about it, Evie? What do you want to call it?"

Ev looked at it. "I don't know. What kind of things can you name them after?"

Carson looked irritated. It was obvious he'd ex-

pected "chrysanthemum." "No proper names, no technological references, no Earth landmarks with 'new' in
front of them, no value judgments."

"What's left?" Ev said.

"Adjectives," I said, "shapes, colors—except for
Green—natural references."

Ev was still examining the plant. "It was growing
out by the sandbar. How about sandpink?"

Carson looked like he was trying to figure out if
there was any way to make sandpink into Crissa. "A
pink's an Earth genus, isn't it, Fin?" he growled at me.

"Yeah," I said. "It'll have to be sandblossom.
Next?"

Bult had names for the rocks, which took forever,
and even he started to look impatient, picking his
binocs up and then putting them down without looking
through them, and nodding at whatever Carson said.

"*Biln,*" Carson said, and I entered it. "Is that everything?"

"We need to name the tributary," I said, pointing
at it. "Bult, do the Boohteri have a name for this river?"

He already had his pony up and was climbing on
it. I had to ask him again.

He shook his head and got down off the pony and
picked up his binocs.

Carson came up beside me. "There's something
wrong," I said.

"I know," he said, frowning. "He's been jittery all
morning."

Bult was looking through his binocs. He took them
down from his eyes and then held them up to his ear.

"Let's go," I said, and went to gather up the specimens. "Wagons ho, Ev!"

"What about the tributary?" Ev said.

"Sandbar Creek," I said. "Come on."

Bult was already going. Carson and I grabbed up the specimens and Carson's binocs, but Bult was already up the bank and heading west between the hills.

"What about the other one?" Ev said.

"Other what?" I said, jamming the specimens in my pack. I slung Carson's binocs around the pommel-bone.

"The other tributary. Do the Boohteri have a name for it?"

"I doubt it," I said, swinging up onto Useless. Carson was having trouble with his pony. If we waited for him, we were going to lose Bult. "Come on," I said to Ev and started after Bult.

"Accordion Creek," Ev said.

"What?" I said, trying to decide which way Bult had gone. I caught a flash of light from his binocs off to the left and urged the pony that way.

"As a name for the other tributary," Ev said. "Accordion Creek, because of the way it folds back and forth."

"No technological references," I said, looking back at Carson. His pony had stopped and was unloading a pile.

"Oh, right," Ev said. "Then how about Zigzag Creek?"

I caught sight of Bult again. He was on top of the next rise, off his pony, looking through his binocs.

"We've already got a Zigzag Creek," I said, waving to Carson to come ahead. "Up north in Sector 250-81."

"Oh," he said, sounding disappointed. "What else means back and forth? Crooked? Tortuous?"

We caught up to Bult, and I unhooked Carson's binocs from the pommelbone and put them up to my eyes, but I couldn't see anything through them but hills and sandblossoms. I upped the resolution.

"Ladder," Ev was muttering beside me. "No, that's technological ... crisscross ... how about Crisscross Creek?"

Well, it was a good try. It wasn't "chrysanthemum," and he'd waited till Carson wasn't there and I was worrying about something else. He was definitely smarter than he looked. But not smart enough.

"Nice try," I said, still scanning the hills with the binocs. "How about Sneaky Creek?" I said as Carson caught up to us. "For the way it tries to slip past you when you're not looking?"

Either Bult had seen what he was looking for through his binocs, or he'd given up. He didn't try to ride ahead for the rest of the afternoon, and after our second rest stop, he put his binocs in his pack and got out his umbrella again. When I asked him the name of a bush during the rest stop, he wouldn't answer me.

Ev wasn't talking either, which was fine because I had a lot to think about. Bult might have calmed down, but he still wasn't levying fines, even though the rest stop had been on a hillside covered with sandblossoms, and two or three times I caught him glaring at me from under his umbrella. When his pony wouldn't get up, he kicked it.

I wondered if irritability was a sign of mating behavior, too, or if he was just nervous. Maybe he wasn't just trying to impress some female. Maybe he was taking us home to meet her.

I called C.J. "I need a whereabout on the indidges," I told her.

"And I need a whereabout on you. What are you doing down in 249-68?"

"Trying to cross the Tongue," I said. "Are there any indidges in our sector?"

"Not a one. They're all up by the Wall in 248-85."

Well, at least they weren't in 248-76.

"Any unusual movements?"

"No. Let me talk to Ev."

"Sure thing. Ask him about the creek we named this morning," I said.

I patched him through and thought about Bult some more, and then asked for another whereabout on the gatecrashers. Wulfmeier still showed on Starting Gate, probably trying to come up with the money to pay his fines.

We got back to the Tongue by late afternoon, but it was still hilly, and the Tongue was too narrow and deep for us to cross. We were close to the Wall—it wound up and down over the hills on the other side— and apparently in a shuttlewren's territory again. Ev alternated between watching it make its rounds and trying to shoo it away so Bult couldn't harpoon it.

Bult headed south, winding up over the tops of hills about like the Wall. I shouted ahead to Carson that it was too steep for the ponies, and he nodded and said something to Bult. Bult plodded on, and ten minutes later his pony keeled over in a dead faint.

Ours followed suit, and we sat down and waited for them to recover. Bult took his umbrella halfway up the hill and sat down under it. Carson lay back and put his hat over his eyes, and I got out Bult's purchase orders and went over them again, looking for clues.

"Do you always see shuttlewrens close to the Wall like this?" he asked. He was apparently recovered from the tongue-lashing C.J.'d given him.

"I don't know," I said, trying to remember. "Carson, do we always see shuttlewrens when we're close to the Wall?"

"Mmph," Carson said from under his hat.

"These species that give gifts to their mates," I said to Ev, "what other kinds of courting do they do?"

"Fighting," he said, "mating dances, displays of sexual characteristics."

"Migration?" I said, looking up the hill at Bult. The umbrella was sitting propped against the hill, its lights on. Bult wasn't under it. "Where's Bult?"

Carson sat up, putting his hat on. "Which way?"

I stood up. "Over there. Ev, tie up the ponies."

"They're still out cold," he said. "What's going on?"

Carson was already halfway up the hill. I scrambled after him.

"Up this gully," he said, and we clambered up it. It led up between two hills, a trickle of water at the bottom, and then opened out. Carson signaled me to wait and went up a hundred meters.

"What is it?" Ev said, coming up behind me, panting. "Has something happened to Bult?"

"Yeah," I said. "Only he doesn't know it yet."

Carson was back. "Just like we thought," he said. "Dead end. What say you go up there"—he pointed—"and I go around that way?"

"And we meet in the middle," I said, nodding. I headed up the side of the gully with Ev behind me. I ran along the crest of the hill in a half crouch, and then dropped to all fours and crawled the rest of the way.

"What is it?" Ev whispered. "A nibbler?" He looked excited.

"Yeah," I whispered back. "A nibbler."

He pulled his knife out.

"Put that away," I hissed at him. "You're liable to fall on it and kill yourself." He put it away. "Don't worry. It's not dangerous unless it's doing something it shouldn't."

He looked confused.

"Down," I said, and we crawled out onto a ledge looking down on the space where the gully widened out. Below us, I could see the flattened area of a gate and a lean-to made of a tarp on sticks. In front of it was Bult.

A man was standing half under the tarp, holding out a handful of rocks to Bult. "Quartz," the man said. "It's found in igneous outcroppings, like this." He reached forward to show Bult a holo, and Bult stepped back.

"You ever seen anything like this around here?" the man said, holding up the holo.

Bult took another step backward.

"It's only a holo, you moron," the man said, holding it out to Bult. "Did you ever see anything like this around here?" and Carson came strolling into the clearing, carrying his pack.

He stopped short. "Wulfmeier!" he said, sounding surprised and amused. "What on hell are you doing on Boohte?"

"Wulfmeier," Ev breathed beside me. I put my finger to my lips to shush him.

"What's that?" Carson said, pointing at the holo. "A postcard?" He walked up next to Bult. "My pony wandered off, and I came looking for him. Same as Bult. How about you, Wulfmeier?"

I wished I could see Wulfmeier's face from where we were. "Something went wrong with my gate," he said, taking a step back under the tarp and looking be-

hind him. "Where's Fin?" he said, and lowered his hand
to his side.

"Right here," I said, and jumped down. "Wulfmeier," I said, holding out my hand. "Fancy meeting
you here. Ev," I called up, "come on down here and
meet Wulfmeier."

Wulfmeier didn't look up. He looked at Carson,
who'd moved off to the side. Ev landed on all fours and
stood up quickly.

"Ev," I said, "this is Wulfmeier. We go way back.
What are you doing on Boohte? It's restricted."

"I told Carson," he said, looking warily from one to
the other of us, "something must have gone wrong with
my gate. I was trying to get to Menniwot."

"Really?" I said. "We had a verify that you were on
Starting Gate." I walked over to Bult. "What you got
there, Bult?"

"I was emptying out my boot, and Bult wanted to
see it," Wulfmeier said, still watching Carson.

Bult handed me the chunks of quartz. I examined
them. "Tch, tch, taking of souvenirs. Bult, looks like
you're going to have to fine him for that."

"I told you, I got them in my shoe. I was walking
around, trying to figure out where I was."

"Tch, tch, tch, leaving footprints. Disturbance of
land surface." I went over to the gate and peered underneath it. "Destruction of flora." I leaned inside the
gate. "What's wrong with it?"

"I got it fixed," Wulfmeier said.

I stepped inside, and came back out again. "Looks
like dust, Carson," I said. "We have a lot of trouble with
dust. Does it get in the chips? He better check it while
we're here, just in case."

Wulfmeier glanced back at the lean-to and over at

Ev, and then back at Carson. He moved his hand away from his side.

"Good idea," he said. "I'll get my stuff."

"Better not," I said. "You wouldn't want to overload the gate. We'll send it along afterward." I went up to the gate controls. "Where'd you say you were trying to go? Menniwot?"

He opened his mouth to say something and then closed it. I asked for coordinates and fed the data into the gate. "That should do it," I said. "You shouldn't end up here again."

Carson walked him over to the gate, and he stepped inside. His hand dropped to his side again, and I hit activate and got out of the way.

Carson was already back at the lean-to, rummaging through Wulfmeier's stuff.

"What'd he have?" I said.

"Ore samples. Gold-bearing quartz, argentite, platinum ore." He leafed through the holos. "Where'd you send him?"

"Starting Gate," I said. "Speaking of which, I better go tell them he's coming. And that somebody's been messing with Big Brother's arrest records. Bult, figure up the fines on this stuff, and we'll send 'em special delivery. Come on," I said to Ev, who was standing there looking at the place where the gate had been like he wished there'd been a fight. "We've gotta call C.J."

We started down the gully. "You were great!" Ev said, scrambling over rocks. "I couldn't believe you faced him down like that! It was just like in the popups!"

We came out of the gully and down the hill to where he'd tied the ponies. They were still lying down.

"What'll happen to Wulfmeier on Starting Gate?" he asked while I wrestled the transmitter off Useless.

"He'll get fined for faking his location and disturbing land surface."

"But he was gatecrashing!"

"He says he wasn't. You heard him. There was something wrong with his gate. He'd have to have been drilling, trading, prospecting, or shooting luggage for Big Brother to confiscate his gate."

"What about those rocks he was giving Bult? That's trading, isn't it?"

I shook my head. "He wasn't giving them to Bult. He was asking if he'd ever seen anything like them. At least he wasn't pouring oil on the ground and lighting it like the last time we caught him with Bult."

"But that's prospecting!"

"We can't prove that either."

"So he gets fined, and then what?" Ev said.

"He'll scrounge up the money to pay the fines, probably from some other gatecrasher who wants to know where to look, and then he'll try again. Up north, probably, now that he knows where we are." Up in Sector 248-76, I thought.

"And you can't stop him?"

"There are four people on this whole planet, and we're supposed to be surveying it, not chasing after gatecrashers."

"But—"

"Yeah. Sooner or later, there'll be one we won't catch. I'm not worried about Wulfmeier—the indidges don't like him, and anything he gets he'll have to find himself. But not all of the gatecrashers are scum. Most of them are people looking for a better place to starve, and sooner or later they'll figure out where a silver mine is from our terrains, or they'll talk the indidges into showing them an oil field. And it'll be all over."

"But the government—what about the regs? What about—"

"Preserving the indigenous culture and the natural ecology? Depends. Big Brother can't stop a mining or drilling operation without sending forces, which means gates and buildings and people taking excursion trips to see the Wall, and forces to protect *them*, and pretty soon you've got Los Angeles."

"You said it depends," Ev said. "On what?"

"On what they find. If it's big enough, Big Brother'll come to get it himself."

"What'll happen to the Boohteri?"

"The same thing that always happens. Bult's a smart operator, but not as smart as Big Brother. Which is why we're putting the money from those out-of-stocks in the bank for him. So he'll have a fighting chance."

I punched send. "Expedition calling King's X. Come in, King's X." I grinned at Ev. "You know, there *was* something wrong with Wulfmeier's gate."

C.J. came on, and I told her to send a message through the gate to Starting Gate and handed her over to Ev so he could fill her in on the details. "Fin was great!" he said. "You should have seen her!"

Bult and Carson were back. Bult had his log out and was talking into it.

"You find anything?" I said.

"Holos of anticlines and diamond pipes. Couple cans of oil. A laser."

"What about the ore samples? Were they indigenous?"

He shook his head. "Standard Earth samples." He

looked at Bult, who'd stopped tallying fines and was going up the hill to get his umbrella. "At least now we know why Bult was leading us down here."

"Maybe." I frowned. "I got the idea he was just as surprised to see Wulfmeier as we were. And Wulfmeier was definitely surprised to see us."

"He'd probably told Bult to sneak off and meet him after dark," he said. "Speaking of which, we'd better get going. I don't want Wulfmeier to come back and find us still here."

"He's not coming back for a while," I said. "He's got a loose T-cable. It'll fall off by the time he gets to Starting Gate."

He smiled. "I still want to make it to the other side of the Wall by tonight."

"If Bult'll let us cross the Tongue," I said.

"Why wouldn't he? He's already had his conference with Wulfmeier."

"Maybe," I said, but Bult didn't go half a klom before he led the ponies across, and not a word about *tssi mitss, e* or otherwise, which shot my theory to pieces.

"You know the best part about that scene back there with Wulfmeier?" Ev said as we splashed across and headed south again. "The way you and Carson worked together. It's even better than on the pop-ups."

I'd watched that pop-up last night. We'd caught Wulfmeier threatening the accordion and come out punching and kicking, lasers blazing.

"You don't even have to say anything. You both know what the other one's thinking." Ev gestured expansively. "On the pop-ups they show you working together, but this was like you were reading each other's minds. You do what the other one wants you to do without even being told. It must be great to have a partner like that."

"Fin, where on hell do you think you're going?" Carson said. He was off his pony and untying the cameras. "Stop jabbering about mating customs and come help me. We're camping here."

It wasn't a bad place to camp, and Bult was back to fining us, or at least me, for every step I took, but I was still worried. Carson's binocs disappeared again, and Bult paced back and forth between the three of us while we were setting up camp and eating supper, giving me murderous looks. After supper he disappeared.

"Where's Bult?" I asked Carson, looking out into the darkness for Bult's umbrella.

"Probably looking for diamond pipes," Carson said, huddling next to the lantern. It was chilly again, and there were big clouds over the Ponypiles.

I was still thinking about Bult. "Ev," I asked, "do any of these species of yours get violent as part of their courtship rituals?"

"Violent?" Ev said. "You mean, toward their mate? Bull zoes sometime accidently kill their mates during the mating dance, and spiders and praying mantis females eat the male alive."

"Like C.J.," Carson said.

"I was thinking more of violence against something else, to impress the female," I said.

"Predators sometimes kill prey to present to the female as a gift," Ev said, "if you'd call that violence."

I would, especially if it meant Bult was leading us into a nibbler's nest or over a cliff so he could dump our carcasses at his girlfriend's feet.

"Fahrrr," Bult said, looming out of the darkness. He dumped a big pile of sticks in front of us. "Fahrrr," he said to Carson, and squatted to light it with a chemical igniter. As soon as it was going, he disappeared again.

"Rivalry among males is common in almost all mammals," Ev said, "elephant seals, primates—"

"Homo sap," Carson said.

"Homo sapiens," Ev said, unruffled, "elk, woodcats. In a few cases they actually fight to the death, but in most it's symbolic combat, designed to show the female who's stronger, more virile, younger—"

Carson stood up.

"Where are you going?"

"To run meteorologicals. I don't like the looks of those clouds over the Ponypiles." You couldn't see the clouds over the Ponypiles, it was so dark, and he'd already run meteorologicals. I'd watched him while we were setting up camp. I wondered if he was worried about Bult and had gone to check on him, but Bult was right here, with another armful of sticks.

"Thanks, Bult," I said. He glared at Ev and then at me again and walked off, still carrying the sticks.

I stood up.

"Where are you going?" Ev said.

"To run a whereabout on Wulfmeier. I want to make sure he made it to Starting Gate." I pulled his pop-up out of my boot and tossed it to him. "Here. Tight Pants and Fancy Mustache'll keep you company."

I went over to the equipment. Carson was nowhere to be seen. I got the log and called up Bult's fines. "Breakdown by day," I said. "Secondary breakdown by person," and watched it for a while, thinking about Bult and the binocs and Ev's mating customs.

When I got back to the fire, Ev was sitting in front

of an officeful of terminals, which didn't look much like a Findriddy and Carson adventure.

"What's that?" I said, sitting down beside him.

"Episode One. That's you," he said, pointing at one of the females.

I wasn't wearing tight pants in this one. I was wearing a skimpy little skirt and one of C.J.'s shirts, landing lights and all, and talking into a screen with a geological on it.

Carson strolled into the office in his luggage vest, fringed pants, and a pair of boots the nibblers wouldn't have even had to bite through. His mustache was slicked down and curled up, and all the females simpered at him like he was a buck with big horns.

"I'm looking for someone to go with me to a new planet," he said, his eyes sweeping the room and coming to rest on Skimpy Skirt. Music from somewhere under the terminals started to play, and everything went pinkish. Carson walked over to her desk and stood over her, looking down her blouse.

After a while he said, "I'm looking for someone who longs for adventure, who's not afraid of danger." He held out his hand, and the music got louder. "Come with me," he said.

"Is that how it was?" Ev said.

Well, my shit, of course it wasn't like that. He'd swaggered in, sat down at my desk, and propped his muddy boots up on it.

"What are you doing here?" I'd said. "You run up too many fines again?"

"Nope," he said, grabbing for my hand. "I wouldn't mind running up a few more fraternizing with the sentients, though. How about it?"

I yanked my hand free. "What are you really doing here?"

"I'm looking for a partner. New planet. Surface survey and naming. Any takers?" He grinned at me. "Lots of perks."

"I'll bet," I said. "Dust, snakes, dehyde food, and no bathrooms."

"And me," he said with that smug grin. "Garden of Eden. Wanta come?"

"Yeah," I said, watching the pop-up go pinker. "That's how it was."

"Come with me," Carson said again to Skimpy Skirt, and she stood up and gave him her hand. A draft from somewhere started blowing her hair and her skimpy skirt.

"It'll be uncharted territory," he said, looking in her eyes.

"I'm not afraid," she said, "as long as I'm with you."

"What on hell's *that* supposed to be?" Carson said limping up.

"The way you and Fin met," Ev said.

"And I suppose those landing lights are supposed to be Fin's?"

"You finish your meteorologicals?" I cut in before he could say anything about not being able to tell I was a female half the time.

"Yeah," he said, warming his hands over the fire. "Supposed to rain in the Ponypiles. I'm glad we're heading north tomorrow." He looked back at Carson and Skimpy Skirt, who were still holding hands and looking sappy-eyed at each other. "Evie, which adventure did you say this was supposed to be?"

"It's when you first met," Ev said. "When you asked Fin to be your partner."

"*Asked* her?" Carson said. "My shit, I didn't ask her. Big Brother said my partner had to be a female, for gender balance, whatever on hell that is, and she was the only female in the department who knew how to run terrains and geologicals."

"Fahrrr," Bult said and dumped his load of sticks on Carson's bad foot.

Expedition 184: Day 3

I hauled my bedroll out by the ponies so I didn't have to listen to Carson, and in the morning I said, "Come on, Ev, you're riding with me. I want to hear all about mating customs from you."

"Chilly around here this morning," Carson said.

I strapped the camera on Useless and cinched it tight.

"I don't like the look of those clouds," Carson said, looking at the Ponypiles. They were covered with low clouds that were spreading out. Half the sky was overcast. "It's a good thing we're heading north."

"Sahhth," Bult said, pointing south. "Brik."

"I thought you said there was a break north of here," Carson said.

"Sahtth," Bult said, glaring at me.

I glared back.

"I don't like the way he's acting," Carson said. "He was gone half the night, and this morning he left a bunch of dice in my bedroll. And Evie says his pop-up's missing."

"Good," I said, climbing up on Useless. "Ev, tell me again about what males do to impress their females."

Bult led us south most of the morning, keeping close to the Tongue, even though the Wall was at least two kloms to the west and there was nothing between us and it but one sandblossom and a lot of pink dirt.

Bult kept sending murderous glances back at me, and kicking his pony to make it go faster. Not only did it, our ponies keeping up with it, but they didn't keel over once all morning. I wondered if Bult had been faking rest stops the way we did dust storms. And what else he'd been faking.

Around noon, I gave up waiting for a rest stop and hauled dehydes out of my pack for lunch, and right after we ate, we came to a creek, which Bult crossed without even looking in, and a handful of silvershims. The whole sky was gray by then, so they didn't look like much.

"Sorry the sun's not out," I told Ev. I looked at their grayish leaves, hanging limp and dusty. "They don't look much like the pop-ups, do they?"

"I'm sorry I lost the pop-up," Ev said. "I put it under my bedroll instead of in my boot." He hesitated. "You didn't know that was how you got chosen to be Carson's partner, did you?"

"Are you kidding?" I said. "That's how Big Brother always does things. C.J. got picked because she was one-sixteenth Navajo." I looked ahead at Carson.

"Why did you come to Boohte?" Ev said.

"You heard the man," I said. "I wanted adventure, I wasn't afraid of danger, I wanted to be famous."

We rode on a ways. "Is that really why?" Ev said.

"Let's change the subject," I said. "Tell me about mating customs. Did you know there's a fish on Starsi that's so dumb it thinks it's being courted when it's not?"

A half a klom after the silvershims, Bult turned west toward the Wall. It bulged out to meet us, and where it did, a whole section was down, a heap of shiny white rubble with high-water marks on it. A flood must've taken it out, even though it was an awfully long way from the Tongue.

Bult led us over the break and, finally, north, keeping next to the Wall all the way back up to the creek we'd crossed. Ev was excited about seeing the front side of the Wall, even though only a few of the chambers looked like they'd been lived in lately, and even more excited about a shuttlewren that tried to divebomb us riding through the break.

"Their territory obviously involves the Wall in some way," he said, leaning sideways to get a look inside. "Have you ever seen one of their nests in the chambers?"

If he leaned over any farther he was going to fall off his pony. "Rest stop!" I called up to Carson and Bult, and pulled back on the reins. "Come on, Ev," I said, and dismounted. "It's against regs to go inside the chambers, but you can peek in."

He looked up ahead at Bult, who had his log out and was glaring back at us. "What about the fine for leaving footprints?"

"Carson can pay it," I said. "Bult hasn't fined him in two days." I went over to a chamber and looked inside the door.

They're not real doors, more like a hole poked in

the middle of the side, and there's no floor either. The sides curve up like an egg. There was a bunch of sandblossoms laid out on the bottom of this one, and in the middle of it one of the American flags Bult had bought two expeditions ago.

"Courtship ritual," I said, but Ev was looking up at the curved ceiling, trying to see if there was a nest. "There are several species of birds that nest in the homes of other species. The panakeet on Yotata, the cuckoo."

We started back to the ponies. It was starting to sprinkle. Up ahead, Bult was getting his umbrella out of his pack and putting it up. Carson was off his pony stomping back to us. "Fin, what on hell do you think you're doing?" he said when he got up to us.

"Taking a rest stop," I said. "We haven't had one all day."

"And we're not going to. We're finally heading north." He took hold of Useless's reins and yanked him forward. "Ev, you stay back here and bring up the rear. Fin's coming up to ride with me."

"I like it back here," I said.

"Too bad," he said, and dragged my pony forward. "You're riding with me. Bult, you lead. Fin and I are riding together."

Bult gave me a murderous glance and lit up his umbrella. He crossed the creek and then rode up along it, going west.

"Now, get on," Carson said and mounted his pony. "I want to be away from the mountains by nightfall."

"And that's why I have to ride with you," I said, swinging my leg up, "so I can tell you which way's north? It's that way."

I pointed north. There was a high bluff in that direction, and between it and the Ponypiles a strip of flat grayish-pink plain, splotched here and there with whitish and dark patches. Bult was heading catty-corner across the flat, still following the stream, his pony leaving deep pawprints in the soft ground.

"Thanks," Carson said. "The way you been acting, I didn't figure you knew which end was up, let alone north."

"What on hell's that supposed to mean?"

"It means you haven't been paying attention to anything since Evelyn showed up and started talking about mating customs. I'd've thought you'd've run out of species by now."

"Well, we haven't," I snapped.

"You're supposed to be surveying, not listening to the loaners. In case you haven't noticed, we're in uncharted territory, we don't have any aerials, Bult's half a klom ahead of us—" He pointed up ahead.

Bult's pony was drinking out of the stream. It was still sprinkling, but Bult turned off his umbrella and collapsed it.

"—and who knows where he's going. He could be leading us into a trap. Or around in circles till the food runs out."

I looked ahead at Bult. He'd crossed the creek and ridden a little way up the other side. His pony was taking another drink.

"Maybe Wulfmeier's back and Bult's leading us straight to him. And you haven't looked at a screen all morning. You're supposed to be running subsurfaces, not listening to Evie Darling talk about sex."

"Listening to him is one hell of a lot more fun than listening to you tell me how to do my job!" I kicked the log on and asked for a subsurface. Up ahead, Bult's pony was stopped and drinking again. I looked down at the stream. Where it cut the low banks, the rock looked like mudstone. "Cancel subsurface," I said.

"You haven't been paying attention to anything," Carson said. "You lose the binocs, you lose the pop-up—"

"Shut up," I said, looking at the bluff, backing the full length of the plain. The plain tilted slightly to its base. "Terrain," I said. "No. Terrain cancel." I looked out at the closest whitish patch. Where the drops of rain were sticking to it, it was pocked with pink.

"You were supposed to keep the pop-up in your boot. If Bult gets hold of it—"

"Shut up," I said. Where Bult's pony had walked there were fifteen-centimeter-deep pawprints in the grayish-brown dirt. The ones up ahead were dark on the bottom.

"If you'd have been paying attention, you'd have realized Wulfmeier—" Carson was saying.

"My shit!" I said, "Dust storm!" and jammed the disconnect. "Shit."

Carson jerked around in the saddlebone as if he expected to see a dust tantrum roaring down on him, and then jerked back and stared at me.

"Subsurface," I said to the terminal. I pointed at the pony's pawprints. "Off-line, and no trace."

Carson stared at the pawprints. "Is everything off?" he said.

"Yes," I said, checking the cameras to make sure.

"Are you running a subsurface?"

"I don't have to," I said, waving at the plain. "It's right there on top. Shit, shit, shit."

Evelyn rode up. "What is it?" he asked.

"I knew he was up to something," Carson said,

looking ahead at Bult. He was off his pony and squatting down at the edge of a dark patch. "I *told* you I thought he was leading us into a trap."

"What *is* it?" Ev said, pulling his knife out. "Nibblers?"

"No, it's a couple of royal saps," Carson said. "Was the log on?"

"Of course it was on," I snapped. "This is uncharted. Terrain, off-line and no trace," I said, but I already knew what it was going to show. A bluff backing a tilted plain. Mudstone. Salt. Seepage. A classic anticline, just like in Wulfmeier's holos. Shit, shit, shit.

"What *is* it?" Evelyn said.

The terrain came up on the screen. "Subsurface overlay," I said.

"Nahtth," Bult called.

I looked up. He had his umbrella up and was pointing with it at the bluff.

"The sneak," Carson said. "Where's he leading us now?"

"We've got to get out of here," I said, scanning the subsurface. It was worse than I thought. The field was fifteen kloms square, and we were right in the middle of it.

"He wants us to follow him," Carson said. "He probably wants to show us a gusher. We've got to get out of here."

"I know," I said, scanning the subsurface. The salt dome went the whole length of the bluff and all the way to the foot of the Ponypiles.

"What do we do?" Carson said. "Go back to the Wall?"

I shook my head. The only sure way out of this was the way we'd come, but the ponies wouldn't backtrail, and the subsurface showed a secondary fault south of the creek. If we went off at an angle we were liable to run into seep, and we obviously couldn't go north.

"Distance overlay," I said. "Off-line and no trace."

"We can't stay off-line all day," Carson said. "C.J.'s already suspicious."

"I *know*," I said, looking desperately at the map. We couldn't go west. It was too far, and the subsurface showed seepage that way. "We've got to go south," I said, pointing at the foothills of the Ponypiles. "We need to get up on that spur so we'll be up above the natural table."

"Are you sure?" Carson said, coming around to look at the screen.

"I'm sure. The rocks are gypsum." Which is frequently associated with an anticline. Shit, shit, shit.

"And then what? Go up into the Ponypiles in that weather?" He pointed at the low clouds.

"We've got to go somewhere. We can't stay here. And any other way's liable to lead us straight into Oklahoma."

"All right," he said, getting up on his pony. "Come on, Ev. We're going."

"Shouldn't we wait for Bult?" Ev said.

"My shit, no. He's already gotten us in enough trouble. Let him find his own way out. That goddamn Wulfmeier. You lead," he said to me, "and we'll follow you."

"You stay right behind me," I said, "and holler if you see something I don't."

Like an anticline. Like an oil field.

I looked at the screen, wishing it would show a path for us to follow, and started slowly across the plain, watching for seep and hoping the ponies wouldn't suddenly go in knee-deep. Or decide to keel over.

It started to drizzle, and then rain, and I had to wipe the screen off with my hand. "Bult's following us," Carson said when we were halfway to the spur.

I looked back. He had his umbrella down and was kicking his pony to catch up.

"What are we going to tell him?" I said.

"I don't know," he said. "Damn Wulfmeier. This is all his fault."

And mine, I thought. I should have recognized the signs in the terrain. I should have recognized the signs in Bult.

The ground turned paler, and I ran a geological and got a mix of gypsum and sulfur in with the mudstone. I wondered if I could risk turning the transmitter back on, and about that time Useless stepped in seep over his paw. It started to drizzle again.

It took us an hour and a half to get out of the oil field and the rain and up into the first hills of the spur. They were gypsum, too, eroded by the wind into flattened and whorled mounds that looked exactly like ponyshit. It apparently hadn't rained as much up here. The gypsum was dry and powdery, and before we'd climbed fifty meters we were coated in pinkish dust and spitting plaster.

I found a stream, and we waded the ponies up it to get the oil off their paws. They balked at the cold water and the incline, and I finally got off and walked Useless, yanking on its reins and cursing it every step of the way up.

Bult had caught up. He was right behind Ev, dragging on his pony's reins and watching Carson thoughtfully. Ev was looking thoughtful, too, and I hoped that didn't mean he'd figured things out, but it didn't look like it. He craned his neck to look at a shuttlewren flying reconnaissance above us.

I needed to get the transmitter back on, but I wanted to make sure we were out of camera range of the anticline first. I dragged Useless up above a clear pool and into a little hollow with rocks on all sides, and unloaded the transmitter.

Ev came up. "I've got to ask you something," he said urgently, and I thought, Shit, I knew he was smarter than he looked, but all he said was "Is the Wall close to here?"

I said I didn't know, and he climbed up the rocks to look for himself. Well, I thought, at least he hadn't said anything about how well Carson and I worked together in a crisis.

I erased the subsurfaces and geologicals and reran the log to see how bad the damage was and then reconnected the transmitter.

"Now what happened?" C.J. said. "And don't tell me it was another dust storm. Not when it was raining."

"It wasn't a dust storm," I said. "I thought it was, but it was a wall of rain. It hit us before I could get the equipment covered."

"Oh," she said, as if I'd stolen her thunder. "I didn't think you could have a dust storm in that mud you were going through."

"We didn't," I said. I told her where we were.

"What are you doing up there?"

"We got worried about a flash flood," I said. "Did you get the subsurface and terrain?" I asked. "I was working on them when the rain hit."

There was a pause while she checked and I wiped my hand across my mouth. It tasted like gypsum. "No," she said. "There's an order for a subsurface and then a cancel."

"A cancel?" I said. "I didn't cancel anything. That must have happened when the transmitter went down. What about aerials? Have you got anything on the Ponypiles?" I gave her our coordinates.

There was another pause. "I've got one east of the Tongue, but nothing close to where you are." She put it on the screen. "Can I talk to Evelyn?"

"He's drying off the ponies. And, no, he hasn't named anything for you yet. But he's been trying."

"He has?" she said, sounding pleased, and signed off without asking anything else.

Ev came back. "The Wall is just the other side of those rocks," he said, wiping dust off his pants. "It goes over the top of the ridge up there."

I told him to go dry off the ponies and reran the log again. The footprints did look like mud, especially with the rain pocking the gray-brown dirt, and it was cloudy, so there wasn't any iridescence. And there wasn't a subsurface. Or an aerial.

But there was me, saying to cancel the subsurface. And the terrain was right there on the log for them to see—the sandstone bluff and the grayish-brown dirt and the patches of evaporated salt.

I looked at the ponies' pawprints. They looked a little like mud, maybe, but they wouldn't when they did the enhances. Which there was no way they wouldn't. Not with C.J. talking about phony dust storms, not when we'd had the transmitter down for over two hours.

I should go tell Carson. I looked down toward the pool, but I didn't see him, and I didn't feel like going to look for him. I knew what he was going to say—that

I should have realized it was an anticline, that I wasn't paying attention, that it was my fault and I was a crummy partner. Well, what did he expect? He'd only picked me because of my gender.

Carson came clambering up the rocks. "I got a look at Bult's log," he said. "He didn't write up any fines down there."

"I know," I said. "I already checked. What'd he say?"

"Nothing. He's sitting up in one of those Wall chambers with his back to the door."

I thought about that.

"His feelings are probably hurt that we didn't pay him for leading us there. Wulfmeier obviously offered him money to show him where there was an oil field." He took off his hat. There was a line of gypsum dust where the brim had been. "I told him we got worried about the rain, that we thought that plain might flood, so we decided to come up here."

"That won't keep him from leading us straight back down there now that it's stopped," I said.

"I told him you wanted to run geologicals on the Ponypiles." He put his hat back on. "I'm gonna go look for a way past the field." He squatted down beside me. "How bad is it?"

"Bad," I said. "You can see the tilt and the mudstone on the log, and I'm on, canceling the subsurface."

"Can you fix any of it?"

I shook my head. "We had the transmitter off too long. It's already through the gate."

"What about C.J.?"

"I told her we ran into rain. She thinks the pawprints are mud. But Big Brother won't."

He came around to look at the screen. "It's that bad?"

"It's that bad," I said bitterly. "Any fool can see it's an anticline."

"Meaning I should've noticed it," he said, bristling. "I wasn't the one dawdling behind talking about sex." He threw his hat down on the ground. "I told you he was going to louse up this expedition."

"Don't you dare blame this on Ev!" I said. "He wasn't the one yelling at me for half an hour while the scans got the whole damned anticline on film!"

"No, he was the one busy noticing birds! And watching pop-ups! Oh, he's been a lot of use! The only thing he's done this whole expedition is try to get a jump out of you!"

I slammed the erase button, and the screen went black. "How do you know he hasn't already gotten one?" I stomped past him. "At least Ev can tell I'm a female!"

I stormed down the rocks, so mad I could have killed him, fine or no fine, and ended up sitting on a gypsum ponypile next to the pool, waiting for him to go off and look for a way down.

After a few minutes he did, clambering up beside the stream without a glance in my direction. I saw Ev come down from the Wall and say something to him. Carson barged past him, and went out along the spur, and Ev stood there staring after him, looking bewildered, and then looked down at me.

He was right about one thing, in all his talk about mating customs. When the hardwiring kicks in, it overrides rational thought, all right. And common sense. I was mad at myself for not seeing the anticline and madder at Carson, and half-sick about what was going to happen when Big Brother saw that log. And I was covered with dried-on gypsum dust and oil and reeking of ponypiles. And, on the pop-ups, my face was always washed.

But that was no reason to do what I did, which was to strip off my pants and shirt and wade into that pool. If Bult saw me I'd be fined for polluting a waterway and Carson would have killed me for not running an f-and-f check first, but Bult was sulking up in the Wall, and the water was so clear you could see every rock on the bottom. It spilled down over rounded boulders into the pool and poured out through a carved-out spout below.

I waded out to the middle, where it was chest-deep, and ducked under.

I stood up, scrubbed gypsum plaster off my arms, and ducked under again. When I came up, Ev was leaning against my gypsum ponypat.

"I thought you were up at the Wall watching shuttlewrens," I said, smoothing back my hair with both hands.

"I was," he said. "I thought you were with Carson."

"I was," I said, looking at him. I sank into the water, my arms out. "Have you figured out the shuttle-wrens' courtship ritual?"

"Not yet," he said. He sat down on the rock and took his boots off. "Did you know the mer-apes on Chichch mate in the water?"

"You sure know a hell of a lot of species," I said, treading water. "Or do you just make them up?"

"Sometimes," he said, unbuttoning his shirt. "When I'm trying to impress a female."

I paddled out to where the water came up to my shoulders and stood up. The current was faster here. It rippled past my legs. "It won't work on C.J. The only thing that'll impress her is Mount Crissa Jane."

He peeled off his shirt. "It's not C.J. I'm trying to impress." He pulled off his socks.

"It's not a good idea to take your boots off in uncharted territory," I said, swimming toward him through the deep water. The current rippled past my legs again.

"The female mer-ape invites the male into the water by swimming toward him," he said. He stripped off his pants and stepped into the water.

I stood up. "Don't come in," I said.

"The male enters the water," he said, wading in, "and the female retreats."

I stood still, peering into the water. I felt the zag, wider this time, and looked where it should be. All I could see was a ripple over the rocks, like air above hot ground.

"Step back," I said, putting my hand up. I walked carefully toward him, trying not to disturb the water.

"Look, I didn't mean to—"

"Slowly," I said, bending down to get the knife out of my boot. "One step at a time."

He looked wildly down at the water. "What is it?" he said.

"Don't make any sudden movements," I said.

"What is it?" he said. "Is there something in the water?" and splashed wildly out of the water and up onto the ponypile.

What looked like a blurring of the current zagged toward me, and I plunged the knife down with a huge splash, hoping I was aiming at the right place.

"What is it?" Ev said.

Now that its blood was spreading in the water, I

could see it, and it was definitely *e*. Its body was longer than Bult's umbrella, and it had a wide mouth. "It's a *tssi mitsse*," I said.

It was also indigenous fauna, and I'd killed it, which meant I was in big trouble. But blood in the water and a fish you couldn't see weren't exactly small trouble. I got away from the blood and out of the water.

Ev was still crouching bare-beamed on the rock. "Is it dead?" he said.

"Yeah," I said, drying off my hair with my shirt and then putting it on. "And so am I." I started pulling the rest of my clothes on.

He got down off the gypsum, looking anxious. "You're not hurt, are you?"

"No," I said, looking in the water and wishing I had been. At least then I could have claimed "self-defense" on the reports.

The blood had spread over the lower half of the pool and was spilling over the spout into the stream. The *tssi mitsse* was drifting toward the spout, too, and I didn't see any activity around it, but I wasn't going back in the water to get it.

I left Ev getting his clothes on and went up to the ponies, which were all lying squeezed in among the rocks. Their paws were still wet, and I thought about us walking them up the stream, and Bult not saying a word. Nobody on this expedition was doing their job.

I took a grappling hook and Bult's umbrella and went down to get the *tssi mitsse* out of the water. Ev was buttoning his shirt and looking embarrassedly at Bult, who was over by the spout, hunched over and looking at the bloody water. I sent Ev to get the holo camera. Bult unfolded himself. He had his log, and he looked pointedly at the umbrella in my hand.

"I know, I know. Forcible confiscation of property," I said. It didn't much matter. Bult's fines were nothing compared to the penalty for killing an indigenous life-form.

The *tssi mitsse* had floated in close to the bank. I hooked it with the umbrella handle and pulled it to the edge and onto the bank, stepping away from it in a hurry, in case it wasn't dead, but Bult went right over to it, unfolded an arm, and started poking his hand into its side.

"*Tssi mitss,*" he said.

"You're kidding," I said. "How big are the big ones?"

It was over a meter long and was perfectly visible now that it was out of the water, with transparent jelly-like flesh that must have the same refraction index as water.

"Tith," Bult said, pulling the mouth back. "Keel bait."

They looked like they could kill bite, all right, or at least take off a foot. There were two long, sharp teeth on either side of its mouth and little serrated ones in between, and that was good. At least it wasn't a harmless algae-eater.

Ev came back with the camera. He handed it to me, looking at the *tssi mitss*. "It's huge," he said.

"That's what you think," I said. "You'd better go find Carson."

"Yeah," he said, and stood there, hesitating. "I'm sorry I jumped out of the water like that."

"No harm done," I said.

I took holos and measurements and brought down the scale to weigh it. When I started to pick it up by the head, Bult said, "Keel bait," and I dropped it with a thud and then took a closer look at its teeth.

Definitely not an algae-eater. The long teeth on either side weren't teeth. They were fangs, and when I ran an analysis of the venom, it ate right through the vial.

I hauled the *tssi mitss* by the tail up the rocks to camp and started in on the reports. "Accidental killing of indigenous fauna," I told the log. "Circumstances—" and then sat and stared at the screen.

Carson came back, scrambling up the rocks from the direction of the pool and stopping short when he saw the *tssi mitss*. "Are you all right?"

"Yeah," I said, looking at the screen. "Don't touch the teeth. They're full of acid."

"My shit," he said softly. "Is this what was in the Tongue when Bult wouldn't let us cross?"

"Nope. This is the small version," I said, wishing he'd get on with it.

"It didn't bite you? You're sure you're all right?"

"I'm sure," I said, even though I wasn't.

He squatted down and looked at it. "My shit," he said again. He looked up at me. "Evie says you were in the pool when you killed it. What on hell were you doing in there?"

"I was taking a bath," I said, looking at the screen.

"Since when do you take baths in uncharted territory?"

"Since I ride all afternoon through gypsum dust," I said. "Since I get covered with oil, trying to wash it off the ponies. Since I find out you can't even tell half the time whether I'm female or not."

He stood up. "So you take off all your clothes and go in swimming with Evie?"

"I didn't take off all my clothes. I had my boots on." I glared at him. "And I don't have to have my clothes off for Ev to be able to tell I'm a female."

"Oh, right, I forgot, he's the expert on sex. Is that what that was down at the pool, some kind of mating dance?" He kicked at the carcass with his bad foot.

"Don't do that," I said. "I've got enough to worry about without having to fill out a form for desecrating remains."

"Worry about!" he said, his mustache quivering. "*You've* got enough to worry about? You know what *I've* got to worry about? What on hell you're going to do next." He kicked the *tssi mitss* again. "You let Wulfmeier open a gate right under our noses, you lead us into an oil field, you take a bath and nearly get yourself killed."

I slammed the terminal off and stood up. "And I lost the binocs! Don't forget that! You want a new partner, is that what you're saying?"

"A new—?"

"A new partner," I said. "I'm sure there are plenty of females to choose from who'd traipse off with you to Boohte the way I did."

"That's what all this is about, isn't it?" Carson said, frowning at me. "It's not about Evie at all. It's about what I said the other night about picking you as a partner."

"You *didn't* pick me, remember?" I said furiously. "*Big Brother* picked me. For gender balance. Only it obviously didn't work because half the time you can't tell which gender I am."

"Well, I sure can right now. You're acting worse than C.J. We been partners for a hundred and eighty expeditions—"

"Eighty-four," I said.

"We've been eating dehydes and putting up with C.J. and getting fined by Bult for eight years. What on hell difference does it make how I picked you?"

"You *didn't* pick me. You sat there with your feet up on my desk and said, 'Wanta come?' and I came, just like that. And now I find out all you cared about is that I could do topographicals."

"All I cared about—?" He kicked the *tssi mitss* again, and a big piece of clear jelly flew off. "I rode into that luggage stampede and got you. I never even looked at any of those female loaners. What do you want me to do? Send you flowers? Bring you a dead fish? No, wait, I forgot, you got one of those for yourself. Lock horns with Evie so that you can tell which one of us is younger and's got both feet? What?"

"I want you to leave me alone. I have to finish these reports," I said, and looked at the screen. "I want you to go away."

Nobody said a word during supper, except Bult, who fined me for dusting off a lump of gypsum before I sat down. It started to rain and all evening Carson kept going out to the edge of the overhang and looking at the sky.

Ev sat in a corner, looking miserable, and I worked on the reports. Bult didn't show any inclination to build any more fires. He sat in the opposite corner watching pop-ups until Carson took it away from him and snapped it shut, and then he opened his umbrella, nearly poking me in the eye with it, and went off up to the Wall.

I wrapped up in my bedroll and worked on the reports some more, but it was too cold. I went to bed. Ev was still sitting in the corner, and Carson was still watching the rain.

I woke up in the middle of the night with water dripping on my neck. Ev was still asleep in his bed-roll, snoring, and Carson was sitting in the corner, with the pop-up spread out in front of him. He was watching the scene in Big Brother's offices, the scene where he asked me to go with him.

Expedition 184: Day 4

In the morning he was gone. It was raining really hard, and the wind had started to blow. There was a stream running through the middle of the overhang and pooling at the back. The foot of Ev's bedroll was already wet.

It was a lot colder, and I figured Carson had gone after firewood, but when I went outside his pony was gone.

I climbed up to the Wall to look for Bult. He wasn't in any of the chambers. I went back down to the pool.

He wasn't there, and the pool wasn't either. Water was pouring everywhere over the rocks, white with gypsum. The ponypile Ev had crouched on was completely covered.

I climbed back up to the Wall and followed it over the ridge. Bult was at the top, looking south toward what you could see of the Ponypiles, which wasn't much, the clouds were so low.

"Where's Carson?" I shouted over the rain.

He looked west and then down at the oil field we'd crossed yesterday. "Dan nah," he said.

"He took one of the ponies," I shouted. "Which way did he go?"

"Nah see liv," he said. "Nah gootbye."

"He didn't say good-bye to anybody," I said. "We've got to find him. You go up along the ridge, and I'll check the way we came up."

But the way we came up was flowing with water, too, and too slick for a pony to have gotten down, and when I went up to the overhang to get Ev, the whole back half was underwater and Ev was piling everything on a damp ledge.

"We've got to move the equipment," he said when he saw me. "Where's Carson?"

"I don't know," I said. I found another overhang higher up, not as deep and tilted up toward the back, and we carried the transmitter and the cameras up. When I went down for the rest of the equipment, I found Carson's log. And his mike.

Bult came back, sopping wet. "Nah fine," he said.

And apparently he doesn't want to be found, I thought, turning the mike over in my hands.

"That overhang isn't going to work," Ev said. "There's water spilling down the side."

We moved the equipment again, into a carved-out hollow away from the stream. It was deep, and the bottom was dry, but by afternoon there was a river running past it, spilling down catty-corner from the ridge, and by morning we'd be cut off from the ponies. And any way out if the water rose.

I went looking again. Water was pouring from both overhangs we'd been in, and there was no way we could get to the other side of the stream, even without *tssi mitss.* I climbed up onto the ridge. It was high enough, but we'd never last out here in the open. I tried not to think about Carson, out in this somewhere with nothing but his bedroll. And no mike.

A shuttlewren dived at my head and around to the Wall again. "Better get in out of this," I said.

I went back down to the hollow and got Ev and Bult. "Come on," I said, picking up the transmitter. "We're moving." I led them up to the ridge and over to the Wall. "In here," I said.

"I thought this was against the regs," Ev said, stepping over the rounded bottom of the door.

"So's everything else," I said. "Including drowning and polluting the waterways with our bodies."

Bult stepped over the door and set his equipment down, and got out his log. "Trespassing on Boohteri property," he said into it.

It took us four trips to get everything up, and then we still had the ponies, which were all lying in a waterlogged pile and wouldn't get up. We had to push them up through the rocks, protesting all the way. It was dark before we got them to the Wall.

"We aren't going to put them in the same chamber with us, are we?" Ev said hopefully, but Bult was already lifting them over the door, paw by paw.

"Maybe we could knock out a door between this passage and the next one," Ev said.

"Destruction of Boohteri property," Bult said, and got out his log.

"At least with the ponies we'll have something to eat," I said.

"Destruction of alien life-form," Bult said into his log.

Destruction of alien life-form. I should get busy on those reports.

"Where was Carson going?" Ev said, as if he'd just remembered he was missing.

"I don't know," I said, looking out at the rain.

"Carson would've waded right in when he saw that thing and killed it," Ev said.

Yeah, I thought, he would have. And then yelled at me for not running an f-and-f check.

"They would have done a pop-up about it," he said, and I thought, Yeah, and I know what that would have looked like. Old Tight Pants without her pants yelling, "Help, help!" and a fish with false teeth lunging up out of the water, and Carson splashing in with a laser and blasting it to hell.

"I told you to get out of the water, and you did," I said. "I would've jumped out myself if I hadn't been so far out."

"Carson wouldn't have," he said. "He would have come to get you."

I looked out at the darkness and the rain. "Yeah," I said. He would have. If he'd known where I was.

Expedition 184: Day 5

It took me all the next day to fill out the reports on the *tssi mitss*, which was probably a good thing. It kept me from standing in the door of the Wall like Ev, staring out at the rain and the rising water.

And it kept me from thinking about Stewart, and how he'd drowned in a flash flood, and about his partner Annie Segura, who'd gone off looking for him and never been found. It kept me from thinking about Carson, washed up somewhere along the Tongue. Or sitting at the bottom of a cliff.

The chamber wasn't much of an improvement on the overhang. The ponies got the runs, and the shuttlewren flew frantically back and forth around our heads. With the rounded floor, there was no place to sit, and the wind kept blowing rain in. Ev and I could've used one of Bult's shower curtains.

Bult didn't need one. He sat under his umbrella watching pop-ups all day. Carson had left it behind, too. I tried to take it away from him, which got me a fine, and then made Ev show him how to make it not take up the whole chamber, but as soon as Ev went back to watching out the door, Bult put it back to full size.

"He's been gone too long," Tight Pants said, swinging up onto her horse, which was in the middle of the ponies. "I'm going to find him."

"It's been nearly twenty hours," the accordion said. "We must report in to Home Base."

"It's been more than twenty-four hours," Ev said, coming back in from the door. "Aren't we supposed to call C.J.?"

"Yeah," I said, and started filling in Form R-28-X, Proper Disposal of Indigenous Fauna Remains. In all those trips up the ridge in the pouring rain, I hadn't thought to bring the *tssi mitss*, which meant I was going to get slapped with another fine.

"Are you going to call her?" Ev said.

I kept filling out the report.

Toward evening C.J. called. "The scans have been showing the same thing all day," she said.

"It's raining. We're waiting it out in a cave."

"But you're all all right?"

"We're fine," I said.

"Do you want me to come pull you out?"

"No."

"Can I talk to Ev?"

"No," I said, looking at him. "He's out with Carson seeing how bad the flooding is." I signed off.

"I wouldn't have told her," Ev said.

"I know," I said, looking at Bult.

Carson and Fin were standing in front of him. "It'll

be uncharted territory," Carson said, holding out his hand.

"I'm not afraid," Fin said, "as long as I'm with you."

"What are you going to do?" Ev said.

"Wait," I said.

Expedition 184: Day 6

The next morning the rain let up a little and then started again. The roof of the chamber developed a leak, right over where we had the equipment piled, and we had to move it over next to the ponies.

It was getting a little crowded. During the night four roadkill had dragged themselves over the door, and the shuttlewren went crazy, wheeling and circling at the top of the chamber, making passes at Ev and me, and at Tight Pants climbing down the cliff.

Bult wasn't watching. He'd gotten up for the hundredth time and gone outside to stand on the ridge.

"What's he doing?" Ev said, watching the shuttlewrens.

"Looking for Carson," I said. "Or a way out of here."

There wasn't any way out. Water was flowing off of every mound, carrying what looked like half the Ponypiles with it, and a raging stream cut across the end of the ridge.

"Where do you think Carson is?" Ev said.

"I don't know," I said. During the night it had occurred to me that Wulfmeier might have gotten his gate fixed and come back to get even. And Carson was alone, no pony, no mike, nothing.

I couldn't tell Ev that, and while I was trying to think of something I could, Ev said, "Fin, come look at this."

He was peering up at the leak in the ceiling. The shuttlewren was making little dives at it.

"It's trying to repair it," Ev said thoughtfully. "Fin, do you still have those parts of the one Bult ate?"

"There wasn't much left," I said, but I dug in my pack and got them out.

"Oh, good," he said, examining the fragments. "I was afraid he'd eaten the beak." He settled down against the wall with them.

The pop-up was still on. Fin was binding up the stub of Carson's foot and bawling. "It's all right," Carson was saying. "Don't cry."

The pop-up went dark and words appeared in the middle of the chamber. The credits. "Written by Captain Jake Trailblazer."

"Look at this," Ev said, bringing over one of the shuttlewren pieces. "See how the beak is flat, like a trowel? Can I run an analysis?"

"Sure." I went over to the door and looked out. Bult was standing on the ridge, where the stream cut across, in the rain.

"I should have figured it out before," Ev said, looking at the screen. "Look at how high the door is. And why would the Boohteri make a curved floor like that?" He stood up and looked at the leak again. "You said you've never seen the Boohteri building one of the chambers?" he said. "Is that right?"

"Yeah."

"Do you remember me telling you about the bowerbird?" he said.

"The one that builds a nest fifty times its size?"

"It's not a nest. It's a courtship chamber."

I couldn't see where this was going. We already knew the indidges used the Wall for courting.

"The male Adelie penguin gives a round stone to the female as a courting gift. But the stone doesn't belong to him. He stole it from another nest." He looked expectantly at me. "Who does that sound like?"

Well, Carson and I'd always said we thought somebody else built the Wall. I looked up at the shuttlewren. "But it's too small to build something like this, isn't it?" I said.

"The bowerbird's bower is fifty times its size. And you said the Wall was only growing by two new chambers a year. Some species only mate every three years, or five. Maybe they work on it several years."

I looked at the curved walls. Three to five years work, and then the imperialistic indidges move in and take it over, knock the door out to make it bigger, put up flags. I wondered what Big Brother was going to say when he heard about this.

"It's just a theory," Ev said. "I need to run probabilities on size and strength and take samples of the Wall's composition."

"It sounds like a pretty good theory," I said. "I've never seen Bult use a tool. Or order one either." The Boohteri word for the wall was "ours," but so was the word for most of Carson's and my wages. And that was Ev's pop-up he'd been watching.

"I'll need a specimen," Ev said, looking speculatively at the shuttlewren making frantic circles around us.

"Go ahead," I said, ducking. "Wring its neck. I'll write up the reports."

"First I want to get this on holo," he said, and spent the next hour filming the shuttlewren poking at the leak. It didn't do anything to it that I could see, but by midmorning the ceiling had stopped leaking, and there was a tiny patch of new-looking white shiny stuff on the ceiling.

Bult came in, with his umbrella and two dead shuttlewrens.

"Give that to me," I said, and snatched one away from him.

He glared at me. "Forcible confiscation of property."

"Exactly." I handed it to Ev. " 'Ours.' You'd better stick it in your boot."

Ev did, and Bult watched him, glaring, and then stuffed the other one in his mouth and went outside. Ev got out his knife and started chipping flakes off of the Wall.

The rain was letting up, and I went out and took a look around. Bult was standing where the stream cut across the ridge, staring up into the Ponypiles. While I watched, he splashed across and went on along the ridge.

The stream must be down, and the pool definitely was. Milky water was still spilling off every surface, but you could see Ev's ponypat rock and the spout at the bottom of the pool. Off to the west the clouds were starting to thin.

I went back up to the ridge. Bult had disappeared.

I went into the chamber and started stuffing things in my pack.

"Where are you going?" Ev said. He'd looked around to make sure it wasn't Bult and then started scraping again.

"To find Carson," I said, fixing the straps so I could put the pack on my back.

"You can't," he said, holding the knife. "It's against the regs. You're supposed to stay where you are."

"That's right." I took off my mike and handed it and Carson's to him. "You wait here till afternoon and then call C.J. to come get you. We're only sixty kloms from King's X. She'll be here in a flash." I stepped over the door.

"But you don't know where he is," Ev said.

"I'll find him," I said, but I didn't have to. He and Bult were coming across the stream talking, their heads bent together. Carson was limping.

I ducked back in the chamber, dumped my pack on the floor, and asked for R-28-X, Proper Disposal of Indigenous Fauna Remains.

"What are you doing?" Ev said. "I want you to take me with you. It's uncharted territory. I don't think you should go look for Carson by yourself," and Carson appeared in the door. "Oh," Ev said, surprised.

Carson stepped over the door and into the middle of the pop-up Bult had been watching. It was raining, and Fin was standing watching two thousand luggage bear down on her. Carson swung into the saddle and galloped toward her.

Carson snapped the pop-up shut. "How wide do you think the field is?" he said to me.

"Eight kloms. Maybe ten. That's how long the bluff is," I said. I handed him his mike. "You lost this."

He put it on. "Are you sure eight is as far as it goes?"

"No, but after that there's caprock, so there won't be any seepage. If we don't run a subsurface, we'll be okay," I said. "Is that where you were, finding a way past it?"

"I want to leave by noon," he said and walked over to Bult. "Come on, we've got work to do."

They squatted in a corner, and Carson emptied out his pockets. Wherever he'd been, he'd collected lots of f-and-f. He had three plants in plastic bags, a holo of some kind of ungulate, and a whole pocketful of rocks.

He ignored us, which didn't bother Ev, who was busy dissecting his specimen. I packed up everything and got the wide-angles on the ponies.

Carson picked up one of the rocks and handed it to Bult. It was a crystal of some kind, transparent with triangular faces. By rights, I should be running a mineralogical to see if it already had a name, but I wasn't about to say anything to Carson, not when he was so pointedly not looking at me.

"Do the Boohteri have a name for this?" Carson asked Bult.

Bult hesitated, as if looking for some cue from Carson, and then said, *"Thitsserrrah."*

"Tchahtssillah?" Carson said.

Books are supposed to begin with a belching "b," but Bult nodded. *"Tchatssarrah."*

"Tssirrroh?" Carson said.

They went on like that for fifteen minutes while I strapped the terminal on my pony and rolled up the bedrolls.

"Tssarrrah?" Carson said, sounding irritated.

"Yahss," Bult said. *"Tssarrrah."*

"*Tssarrrah,*" Carson said. He stood up, went over to my pony, and entered the name. Then he went back to where Bult was squatting and started picking up the plastic bags. "We'll do the rest of these later. I don't want to spend another night in the Ponypiles."

And what was that all about? I thought, watching him put the plants in his pack.

Ev was still working on his specimen. "Come on," I said. "We're leaving."

"Just a couple more holos," he said, grabbing up the camera.

"What's he doing?" Carson said.

"Gathering data," I said.

Ev had to take holos of the outside, too, and scrape a sample of the outside surface.

It was another half hour before he was finished, and Carson acted fidgety the whole time, swearing at the ponies and looking at the clouds. "It looks like it's going to rain," he kept saying, which it didn't. The rain was obviously over. The clouds were breaking up and the puddles were already drying up.

We finally set off a little past midday, Bult and Carson in the lead and Ev bringing up the rear, taking holos of the Wall and the shuttlewren who was supervising our departure.

The stream that had cut across the ridge was already down to a trickle. We followed it down to where it connected with the Tongue, and began following it east.

It made a wide canyon here with room on the far side for ponies. Bult knelt down on the bank and inspected it, though I didn't see how he'd be able to see a *tssi mitss* in the muddy pink water. But they must all have been washed downriver in the flood because he gave the go-ahead and we waded the ponies across and started up the canyon.

After the first klom or so the bank got too rocky to be muddy and the clouds started to drift off. The sun even came out for a few minutes. Ev messed with his specimen, Carson and Bult talked and gestured, deciding which way to go, and I fumed. I was so mad I could've killed Carson. I'd been picturing him washed up in some gulch, half-eaten by a nibbler, for the last three days. And not so much as a word when he came back about how on hell he'd made it through the flood or where on hell he'd been.

We began to climb, and I could hear a faint roar up ahead.

"Do you hear that?" I asked Ev.

He had his head in his screen, working on his shuttlewren theory, and I had to ask him again.

"Yeah," he said, looking up blankly. "It sounds like a waterfall," and a couple of minutes later there was one. It was just a cascade, and not very high, but right above it the river twisted out of sight, so it was a real waterfall and not just a rough section of river, and we'd gotten above where the rain started, so the water ran a nice clear brownish color.

The gypsum piles made a whole series of bubbling zigzag rushes, and it was presentable-looking enough I figured Ev would at least make a try at naming it after C.J., but he didn't even look up from his screen and Carson rode right past it.

"Aren't we gonna name it?" I hollered ahead to him.

"Name what?" he said, as blank as Ev when I'd asked him about the roar.

"The waterfall."

"The water—?" he said, turning fast to look not at the waterfall, which was right in front of him, but up ahead.

"The *water*fall," I said, pointing at it with my thumb. "You know. Water. Falling. Don't we need to name it?"

"Of course," he said. "I just wanted to see what was up ahead first," which I didn't believe for a minute. Naming it hadn't so much as crossed his mind till I said it, and when I'd pointed at it he'd had an expression on his face I couldn't make out. Mad? Relieved?

I frowned. "Carson—" I started, but he'd already twisted around to look at Bult.

"Bult, do the indidges have a name for this?" he said.

Bult looked, not at the waterfall, but at Carson, with a questioning expression, which was peculiar, and Carson said, "He hasn't been this far up the Tongue. Ev, you got any ideas?"

Ev looked up from his screen. "According to my calculations, a shuttlebird could construct a Wall chamber in six years," he said happily, "which matches the mating period of the blackgull."

"What about Crisscross Falls?" I said.

Carson didn't even look annoyed, which was even more peculiar. "What about Gypsum Falls? We haven't used that yet, have we?"

"They'd have to begin building before maturation," Ev said, "which means the mating instinct would have to be activated at birth."

I checked the log. "No Gypsum Falls."

"Good," Carson said and set off again before I even had it entered.

We'd never named a weed that fast, let alone a wa-

terfall, and Ev had apparently forgotten all about C.J.
and sex, unless he thought there'd be plenty of other
waterfalls to pick from. He might be right. I could still
hear the roar of water, even when we went around the
curve in the canyon, and around the next curve it got
even louder.

Bult and Carson had stopped up above the waterfall and were consulting. "Bult says this isn't the
Tongue," Carson said when we came up. "He says it's a
tributary, and the Tongue's farther south."

He hadn't said that. Carson had just told me the
Boohteri hadn't been up this far, and besides, Bult
hadn't opened his mouth. And Carson looked preoccu-
pied, the way Bult had right before the oil field episode.

But Carson was already splashing us back across
the river and up the side of the canyon, not even looking at Bult to see which way he was going. He stopped
at the top. "This way?" he asked Bult, and Bult gave
him that same questioning look and then pointed off up
a hill. And what was he leading us into now? *If* he was
the one leading us.

We were above the gypsum now, the soapy slopes
giving way to a brownish-rose igneous. Bult led us up
a break in another, steeper hill, and toward a clump of
silvershim trees. They were old ones, as tall as pines
and in full leaf. They would have been blinding if the
sun had been out, which it looked like it might be again
in a minute.

"Here're the silvershims you were so anxious to
see," I said to Ev, and after talking to his screen he
raised his head and looked at them.

"They'd look a lot better if we were out in the

sun," I said, and right then it put in an appearance and
lit them up.

"I told you," I said, putting up my hand to shade
my eyes.

Ev looked dazed, and no wonder. They glittered
like one of C.J.'s shirts, the leaves shimmering and re-
flecting in the breeze.

"Not much like the pop-ups, is it?" I said.

"*That's* what gives the Wall its shiny texture!" he
said, and slapped his forehead with the flat of his hand.
"That was the only part I couldn't figure out, what gave
it that shine." He started taking holos. "The shuttlewrens must chew the leaves up."

Well, so much for the silvershims he'd come all the
way to Boohte to see. Was C.J. going to be mad when
she found out Ev had forgotten her and taken up with
some leaf-chewing, plaster-spitting bird!

The ponies had slowed to a crawl, and I would
have been happy to take a rest stop and sit and look at
the trees for a few minutes, but Bult and Carson rode
on through the middle of them. When Bult wasn't looking, I picked a handful of the leaves and handed them
to Ev, but I doubted if Bult would have fined me if he'd
seen me. He was too busy looking ahead at a stream we
were coming to.

It wasn't much bigger than the trickle up on top of
the ridge, and it was coming from the wrong direction,
but Bult claimed it was the Tongue. We started up it,
winding in and out between the trees till the igneous
on either side began to shut them out. It stacked up in
squarish piles like old red bricks, and I grabbed a loose
piece and ran an analysis. Basalt with cinnabar and gypsum crystals mixed in. I hoped Carson knew where he
was going, because there was no room to backtrail here.

The canyon was getting steeper, too, and the ponies started to complain. The stream climbed up in a little series of cascades that chortled instead of roaring, and the banks turned into reddish-brown blocks, as steep as stairs.

The ponies'll never make it, I thought, and wondered if that was what Carson was up to—leading us into some defile so steep we'd have to carry the ponies through it on our shoulders just for spite. Carson'd have to carry his, too, though, and the way he was kicking his and swearing at it I didn't think he was playacting.

Carson's pony stopped and leaned back so far on his rear legs I thought he was going to pitch back onto me. Carson got off and pulled on the reins. "Come on, you beam-headed, rock-brained hind end," he shouted, leaning right in his pony's face, which must have scared him because he dumped a huge pile and started to topple over, but the rock wall stopped him.

"Don't you *dare* try that," Carson bellowed, "or I'll dump you in this stream for the *tssi mitss* to eat. Now, come *on*!" He gave a mighty yank on the reins, and the pony stepped back, dislodged a rock, which went clattering down into the stream, and took off up the steps like he was being chased.

I hoped my pony would get the hint, and he did. He lifted his tail and plopped a big pile. I got off and took hold of his reins. Bult took out his log and looked at Ev expectantly.

"Come on, Ev," I said.

Ev looked up from his screens, blinking in surprise. "Where are we going?" he said, like he hadn't so much as noticed we weren't still meandering through the silvershims.

"Up a cliff," I said. "It's a mating custom."

"Oh," he said, and dismounted. "The shuttlewren's flight range puts the silvershims well within range. I need to run tests on the plaster's composition to make sure, but I can't do that till I get back to King's X."

I knotted the reins tight under Useless's mouth, and whispered, "You lazy, broken-down copy of a horse, I'm going to do everything Carson's ever threatened you with and some he hasn't even thought of, and if you shit one more time before we're out of this canyon, I'll pull that pommelbone right out of your neck."

"What on hell's keeping you?" Carson said, coming back down the steps. He didn't have his pony.

"I'm not carrying this pony," I said.

He sidestepped the piles and got behind Useless and pushed for a while.

"Turn her around," he said.

"It's too narrow," I said. "You know ponies won't backtrail."

"Yeah," he said and took the reins and yanked her around till she was nose to nose with Ev's pony. "Come on, you poor imitation of a cow, let alone a horse," he said, and pulled, and she backed right up the canyon.

"You're smarter than you look," I called after him as he went back for Ev's.

"You ain't seen nothin' yet," he said.

We didn't have any more trouble with the ponies— they hung their heads like they'd been outsmarted and plodded steadily upward, but it still took us the better part of an hour to climb half a klom, and we were going nowhere. The stream shrank to a trickle and half disappeared between the rocks. It obviously wasn't the Tongue, and Carson must have had the same idea, because the next side canyon we came to he led us into it back the direction we'd come.

It was just as steep and twice as narrow. I didn't have to stop and take mineral samples, I just scraped them off with my legs as we rode past. The basalt blocks got smaller and began to look like a brick wall, and between them there were zigzag veins of the triangle-faceted crystals Carson had brought home. They acted like prisms, flashing pieces of the spectrum across the narrow canyon when the sun hit them.

Just about when I'd decided the canyon was going to run into a bricked-up dead end, we climbed up and onto the flat and back into silvershims.

We were on a wide overhang with trees growing right up to the edge, and I could see, off to the right, the Tongue far below and hear the roar of its waterfalls. Carson ignored it and rode off through the middle of the trees, heading straight for the far edge, not even bothering now to pretend Bult was leading.

I was right, I thought, he is leading us over a cliff, and came out of the trees. He'd tied his pony to a trunk and was standing close to the edge, looking out across the canyon. Ev rode up, and then Bult, and we just sat there on our ponies, gawking.

"Well, what do you know?" Carson said, trying to sound astonished. "Will you look at that? It's a waterfall."

That cascade with the gypsum piles was a waterfall. There was no word for what this was, except that it was obviously the Tongue, meandering through the silvershim forests on the far side and then plunging a good thousand meters into the canyon below us.

"My shit!" Ev said and dropped his shuttlewren. "My *shit!*"

My sentiments exactly. I'd seen holos of Niagara

and Yosemite Falls when I was a kid, and they were pretty impressive, but they were only water. This—

"My *shit!*" Ev said again.

We were standing a good five hundred meters above the canyon floor and opposite a rose brick cliff that rose up another two hundred meters. The Tongue leapt out of a narrow V in the top of it and flung itself like a suicide down into the canyon with a roar I should never have mistaken for a cascade, throwing up a billow of mist and spray I could almost feel, and crashing into the swirling green-white water below.

The sun ducked under a cloud and then came out again, and the waterfall exploded like fireworks. There was a double rainbow across the top of the spray, and that one was probably from the water's refracting the sunlight, but the rest of them were from the cliff. It was crisscrossed with veins of the prismatic crystal, and they sparkled and glittered like diamonds, flashing chunks of rainbow onto the cliff, onto the falls, into the air, across the whole canyon.

"My *shit!*" Ev said again, hanging on to his pony's reins like they could hold him up. "That's the most beautiful thing I've ever seen!"

"Lucky us stumbling onto it this way," Carson said, and I turned to look at him. He had his thumbs in his belt loops and was looking smug. "If we'd kept on up that canyon," he said, "we'd have missed it altogether."

Lucky, my boots, I thought. All that dragging us through silvershims and up steps and consulting with Bult like you didn't know where you were going. This is what you were doing while I was waiting for you in the Wall, worried sick. Off chasing rainbows.

He must have found it by following the Tongue, looking for a way around the anticline, and then gone off wandering up cliffs and in and out of side canyons, searching for the best vantage point to show it to us from. If we'd stayed on the Tongue, the way he probably had when he found it, we'd have caught a half glimpse of it around some bend, or heard the roar get louder and guessed what was coming, instead of having it burst on us all at once like some view of rainbow heaven.

"Really lucky!" Carson said, his mustache quivering. "So, what do you want to name it?"

"Name it?" Ev's head jerked around to look at Carson, and I thought, Well, so much for birds and scenery, we're back to sex.

"Yeah," Carson said. "It's a natural landmark. It's gotta have a name. How about Rainbow Falls?"

"*Rainbow* Falls?" I snorted. "It's gotta have a better name than that," I said. "Something big, something that'll give some idea of what it looks like. Aladdin's Cave."

"Can't name it after a person."

"Prism Falls. Diamond Falls."

"Crystal Falls," Ev said, still staring at it.

He'd never get it past them. Chances were Big Brother, ever vigilant, would spot it and send us a pursuant that said Crissa Jane Tull worked on the survey team and the name was ineligible, and this time they'd be able to prove a connection, and we'd get fined to within an inch of our lives.

It was too bad, because Crystal Falls was the perfect name for it. And until Big Brother caught it, Ev would get a lot of jumps out of C.J.

"Crystal Falls," I said. "You're right. It's perfect."

I looked at Carson, wondering if he was thinking

the same thing, but he wasn't even listening. He was looking at Bult, who had his head bent over his log.

"What's the Boohteri name for the waterfall, Bult?" Carson asked, and Bult glanced up, said something I couldn't hear, and looked down at his log again.

I left Ev drooling into the canyon and went over by them, thinking, Great, it's going to end up being called Dead Soup Falls or, worse, "Ours." "What'd he say?" I shouted to Carson.

"Damage to rock surface," Bult said. He was catching up his fines. "Damage to indigenous flora."

I figured he was going to have to add, "Inappropriate tone and manner," but Carson didn't look so much as annoyed. "Bult," he shouted, but only because of the roar, "what do you call it?"

He looked up again and stared vaguely off to the left of the waterfall. I took the opportunity to snatch the log out of his hands.

"The waterfall, you pony-brained nonsentient!" I said, pointing, and he shifted his gaze in the right direction, though who on hell knows what he was really looking at—a cloud maybe, or some rock slung halfway down the cliff.

"Do the Boohteri have a name for the waterfall?" Carson said patiently.

"*Vwarrr*," Bult said.

"That's the word for water," Carson said. "Do you have a name for this waterfall?" and Bult looked at Carson with that peculiar questioning look, and I thought, amazed, he's trying to figure out what Carson wants him to say.

"You said your people had never been in the mountains," Carson said, prompting him, and Bult looked like he'd just remembered his line.

"Nah nahm."

"You can't call it Nah Nahm," Ev said from behind us. "You've got to name it something beautiful. Something grand!"

"Grand Canyon!" I said.

"Something like Heart's Desire," Ev said. "Or Rainbow's End."

"Heart's Desire," Carson said thoughtfully. "That's not bad. Bult, what about the canyon? Do the Boohteri have a name for that?"

Bult knew his line this time. "Nah nahm."

"Crown Jewels Canyon," Ev said. "Starshine Falls."

"It should really be an indidge name," Carson said piously. "Remember what Big Brother said. 'Every effort should be made to discover the indigenous name of all flora, fauna, and natural landmarks.'"

"Bult just told you," I said. "They don't have a name for it."

"What about the cliff, Bult?" Carson said, looking hard at Bult. "Or the rocks? Do the indidges have a name for those?"

Bult looked like he needed a prompter, but Carson didn't seem mad. "What about the crystals?" he said, digging in his pocket. "What did you name that crystal?"

The roaring of the falls seemed to get louder.

"*Thitsserrrah*," Bult said.

"Yeah," Carson said. "*Tssarrrah*. You said Crystal Falls, Ev. We'll name it *Tssarrrah* after the crystals."

The roar got so loud it made me go dizzy, and I grabbed on to the pony.

"Tssarrrah Falls," Carson said. "What do you think, Bult?"

"Tssarrrah," Bult said. "Nahm."

"How about you?" Carson said, looking at me.

Ev said, "I think it's a beautiful name."

I walked over to the edge of the overhang, still feeling dizzy, and sat down.

"That settles it," Carson said. "Fin, you can send it in. Tssarrrah Falls."

I sat there listening to the roar and watching the glittering spray. The sun went in behind a cloud and burst out again, and rainbows darted across and above the cliff like shuttlewrens, sparkling like glass.

Carson sat down beside me. "Tssarrrah Falls," he said. "It was lucky the indidges had a word for those crystals. Big Brother's been wanting us to give more stuff indigenous names."

"Yeah," I said. "Lucky. What does *tssarrrah* mean, did Bult say?"

" 'Crazy female,' probably," he said. "Or maybe 'heart's desire.' "

"How much did you have to bribe him with? Next year's wages?"

"That was what was funny," he said, frowning. "I was going to give him the pop-up since he likes it so much. I figured I might have to give him a lot more than that after the oil field, but I asked him if he'd help, and he said yes, just like that. No fines, nothing."

I wasn't surprised.

"Did you get the name sent?" he said.

I looked at the falls for a long minute. The water roared down, dancing with rainbows. "I'll do it on the way down. Hadn't we better get going?" I said, and stood up.

"Yeah," he said, looking south at where the clouds were accumulating again. "Looks like it's going to rain again."

He held out his hand, and I yanked him to his feet. "You didn't have any business going off like that," I said.

He still had hold of my hand. "You didn't have any business nearly getting yourself killed." He let go of my hand. "Bult, come on, you've got to lead us back down."

"How on hell are we supposed to do that when the ponies won't backtrail?" I said, but Bult's pony walked right through the silvershims and down into the narrow canyon, and ours followed single file without so much as a balk.

"Dust storms aren't the only things being faked around here," I muttered.

Nobody heard me. Carson was up behind Bult, still doing the leading, down the side canyon, back through the one where the ponies had given us so much trouble, and then into another side canyon. I let them get ahead and looked back at Ev. He was bent over his terminal, probably looking at shuttlewren stats. I called C.J.

After I talked to her, I looked ahead and caught a glimpse of the side of the falls. The rainbows were lighting up the sky. Ev caught up to me. "They'll never get it on the pop-ups like it really was," he said.

"No," I said. "They won't."

The canyon widened, and we could see the falls from an angle, the water leaping sideways off the crystal-studded cliff and straight down.

"Speaking of which," Ev said, "what's Carson's first name?"

I'd told Carson he was smart. "What?"

"His first name. I got to thinking that I don't know it. On the pop-ups you never call each other anything but Findriddy and Carson."

"It's Aloysius," I said. "Aloysius Byron. His initials are A.B.C. Don't tell him I told you."

"*His* first name's Aloysius," he said thoughtfully. "And yours is Sarah."

As smart as they come.

"Did you know that in some species the males all compete for the most desirable female?" he said, smiling wryly. "Most of them don't stand a chance, though. She always picks the one who's the bravest. Or the smartest."

"Speaking of which, you were pretty smart to figure out the shuttlewrens built the Wall."

He brightened. "I still have to prove it," he said. "I'm going to have to run content analyses and work/size probabilities when I get back to King's X. And write it up."

"It'll be on the pop-ups, too," I said. "You'll be famous. Ev Parker, Socioexozoologist."

"You think so?" he said, as if it hadn't occurred to him before.

"I know so. A whole episode."

He looked hard at me. "It's you, isn't it? You're the one writing the episodes. You're Captain Jake Trailblazer."

"Nope," I said, "but I know who is." And her initials are C.J.T., I thought. "My shit, you may get a whole series."

The canyon opened out, and we were on another overlook, as big as a field this time, and lower down. Off to one side there was a way down, a slope leading back along the canyon to its floor. Beyond the canyon you could see the plains, pink and lavender. I could see the bluff that backed the anticline off to the east, too far off the scans to notice anything.

"Rest stop," Bult said and got off his pony. He sat down under a silvershim and opened out the pop-up.

"Do you hear that?" Carson said, looking up in the sky.

"It's C.J.," I said. "I told her to come get Ev so he can work on his theory. He's gotta run some tests."

"Is she doing aerials?" he said, looking anxiously back in the direction of the bluff.

"I told her to go south and come in over the Ponypiles, that we needed an aerial of them," I said.

"What about on the way back?"

"Are you kidding? She's going to have Ev with her. She won't be running any aerials with him in the heli. My shit, she probably forgot to do the aerials on the way down, she was so excited."

Carson looked at me questioningly. The heli swooped in and hovered above the field. C.J. jumped down from the bay, ran across to Ev, and practically knocked him down, kissing him.

"What's all that about?" Carson said, watching them.

"Courtship ritual," I said. "I told her Ev named the falls after her. I told her he named it Crystal Falls." I looked at Carson. "It was the only way he was ever going to get a jump. On this planet, anyway."

They were still in a clinch.

"When she finds out what we really named it," Carson said, grinning, "she's gonna be really mad. When are you gonna tell her?"

"I'm not," I said. "That's the name I sent."

He quit grinning. "What on hell did you do that for?"

"The other day Ev almost got a name past me. Crisscross Creek. You were worrying about what Bult was up to, and I was busy trying to load everything on the ponies, and when he asked me what we were going to name that little stream we crossed, I wasn't paying any attention. It wouldn't have gotten past Big Brother, but it got past me. Because I was busy worrying about something else."

Ev and C.J. had come out of their clinch and were looking at the waterfall. C.J. was making squealing noises that practically drowned out the falls.

"Crystal Falls won't get past Big Brother either," Carson said. "And *Tssarrrah* Falls would have."

"I know," I said, "but maybe they'll be so busy yelling at us over naming it that and killing the *tssi mitss* that they'll forget about the oil field."

He stared at Ev. C.J. was kissing him again. "What about Evie?"

"He won't tell," I said.

"What about Bult? How do we know he won't lead us out of these mountains and straight into another anticline? Or a diamond deposit?"

"That's not a problem either. All you've got to do is tell him."

He turned and looked at me. "Tell him what?"

"Can't you tell when somebody's got a crush on you? Making you fires, watching your scenes on the pop-ups over and over, giving you presents—"

"What presents?"

"All those dice. The binocs."

"They were *our* binocs."

"Yeah, well, the indidges seem to have a little trouble with that word. He gave you half a shuttlewren, too. And an oil field."

"*That's* why he said he'd help me with the waterfall." He stopped. "I thought Ev said he was a male."

"He is," I said, grinning. "And apparently he's got

as much trouble telling what sex we are as we did with him."

"He thinks I'm a *female*?"

"It's an easy enough mistake," I said, grinning. I started to walk away.

He grabbed my arm and swung me around to face him. "You're sure you want to do this? We could get fired."

"No, we won't. We're Findriddy and Carson. We're too famous to get fired." I smiled at him. "Besides, they can't. After this expedition, we're going to owe them our wages for the next twenty."

We went over to C.J. and Ev, who were glued together again. "Ev, you and your pony go back with C.J. to King's X," I said. "You've gotta get that theory on the Wall written up."

"Evelyn told me about his theory," C.J. said. I wondered when he'd had the time. "And how he saved you from the *tssi mitss*."

"We're gonna go ahead and finish out the expedition," Carson said, dragging Ev's pony over. "I thought we'd survey the Ponypiles as long as we're here."

We heaved the pony into the bay, and told C.J. to swing west over the Ponypiles and then north on the way home and try to get an aerial.

She wasn't paying any attention. "Take all the time you need surveying," she said, climbing on. "And don't worry about us. We'll be fine." She went forward.

Carson handed Ev his pack. "If you could take holos of the Wall at different places, I'd appreciate it," Ev said. "And samples of the plaster."

Carson nodded. "Anything else we can do?"

Ev looked up at the heli. "You've already done quite a bit." He shook his head, grinning. "Crystal

Falls," he said, looking at me. "I still think we should've named it Heart's Desire."

He climbed up into the bay, and C.J. took off, dipping so close to the ground we both ducked.

"Maybe we did too much," Carson said. "I hope C.J. isn't so grateful she kills him."

"I wouldn't worry about it," I said. The heli circled the canyon like a shuttlewren and swooped down in front of the falls for a last look. They flew off, straight north across the plains, which meant we weren't going to get any aerials.

"We're just postponing the inevitable, you know," he said, looking after the heli. "Sooner or later Big Brother's going to figure out we've been having way too many dust storms, or Wulfmeier'll stumble onto that vein of silver in 246-73. If Bult doesn't figure out what he could get for this place and tell them first."

"I've been thinking about that," I said. "Maybe it wouldn't be as bad as we think. They didn't build the Wall, did you know that? They just moved in afterward, clunked the natives on the head, and took over. Bult'd probably own Starting Gate and half of Earth inside a year."

"And build a dam over the falls," he said.

"Not if it was a national park," I said. "You heard what Ev said about how he'd wanted to see the silvershims and the Wall, especially when they find out who built it. I figure people would come a long way to see something like this." I gestured at the falls. "Bult could charge admission."

"And fine them for leaving footprints," he said. "Speaking of which, what's to stop Bult from getting a crush on you once I tell him I'm not a female?"

"He thinks I'm a male. You said yourself, half the time you can't tell what sex I am."

"And you're never going to let me forget it, are you?"

"Nope," I said.

I went over to where Bult was sitting, watching the pop-up of Carson holding Skimpy Skirt's hand. "Come with me," Carson said.

"Come on, Bult," I said. "Let's get going."

Bult shut the pop-up and handed it to Carson.

"Congratulations," I said. "You're engaged."

Bult got out his log. "Disturbance of land surface," he said to me. "One-fifty."

I climbed up on Useless. "Let's go."

Carson was looking at the falls again. "I still think we should've named it Tssarrrah Falls," he said. He went over to his pony and started rummaging in his pack.

"What on hell are you doing now?" I said. "Let's go!"

"Inappropriate tone and manner," Bult said into his log.

"I wasn't talking to you," I said. "What are you looking for?" I said to Carson.

"The binocs," Carson said. "Have you got 'em?"

"I gave 'em to you," I said. "Now, come on."

He got on his pony and we started off down the slope after Bult. Out beyond the cliff the plain was turning purple in the late afternoon. The Wall curved down out of the Ponypiles and meandered across it, and

beyond it you could see the mesas and rivers and cinder cones of uncharted territory, spread out before me like a present, like a bowerbird's treasures.

"You did not give the binocs back to me," Carson said. "If you lost 'em again—"

About the Author

CONNIE WILLIS has received six Nebula Awards and four Hugo Awards for her short fiction, and the John W. Campbell Award for her first novel, *Lincoln's Dreams*. Her first short story collection, *Fire Watch*, was a *New York Times* Notable Book, and her latest novel, *Doomsday Book*, won the Nebula and Hugo Awards. Ms. Willis lives in Greeley, Colorado, with her family.